KATHI S. BARTON

This is a work of fiction. Names, characters, places, and incidents are products of the author's imagination or are used fictitiously and are not to be construed as real. Any resemblance to actual events, locations, organizations, or persons, living or dead, is entirely coincidental.

World Castle Publishing, LLC
Pensacola, Florida

Paperback ISBN: 9781955086691
eBook ISBN: 9781955086707
First Edition World Castle Publishing, LLC, August 9, 2021
http://www.worldcastlepublishing.com

Licensing Notes

Cover: Karen Fuller
Editor: Maxine Bringenberg

Prologue

Every time Dwayne looked at his brother, he laughed. There was no point in holding back anymore, either. Everyone had seen and heard him react to Gunner and Hodge popping out of the book, so there was no hiding the fact that Sawyer had been the perfect stodge to have pulled this on.

Gunner had told Sawyer to put the book on the floor. Not questioning his brother, he did just what he'd asked him to do. Then Sawyer, falling hook line and sinker for whatever reason Gunner had told him to say abracadabra over it, was just too funny. Gunner and Hodge had just appeared, something akin to being sprinkled from the ceiling. Sawyer had leapt back from them, fallen over the coffee table, breaking it, and screaming like a little girl seeing a spider. Dwayne would forever hear a child scream like that and think of this day.

"Keep laughing it up, and I'll give you a good reason to be sobbing over your supper later." He couldn't help it. Dwayne laughed all the harder. "I'm going to knock the shit out of you."

"Behave, the two of you. It was fun. You have to admit, there haven't been that many fun things around here of late. Not with us trying to hunt down a killer, people getting their asses shot to fuck, and things like recording devices showing up in the strangest places." Dwayne noticed that his mom didn't say anything to the girls for their potty mouth, as she called it. He thought that Andi had the worst of it. Hearing it from men all the time was something he could understand. Sometimes he'd forget she was a woman.

Andi didn't look manly or anything like that. Nor did she have a haircut that would make it difficult to tell what gender she was from behind. Her hair was as beautiful as any sunset he'd ever witnessed, and her figure in those tight pants that women wore nowadays was perfect on her body. Not that he was looking too hard.

"I need to ask you a couple of questions." Dwayne told Chandler he was all ears. "I don't want to alarm you, but you have a family following you around. A woman, two children, and a man. None of them seem to be upset or anything like that. They're new to you. I mean, all of us have a ghost or two hanging around, with the exception of Andi. But this family is new to you."

"Why not Andi?" He said that neither of them knew. "So, you think she's not ever hurt anyone or caused their deaths? I haven't either. Not that I know of. And this couple, what do they look like? What I mean is, my age? Older? Tell me something so I can remember them."

"They're all four dead, of course. I'm thinking some sort of toxin killed them." Dwayne watched as his brother had a conversation with, he assumed, one of them. "Carbon poisoning. You do know them in a way. You tried to save them when you came upon their car. Do you remember that?"

"Yes." He looked in the direction his brother was still looking. "If you can hear me, I'm still trying to reach your sister, missus. The number I found in your home was old and no longer assigned. The police have your cell phone. As soon as they turn it over to me for the few minutes they said I could have, I'll call her."

"What happened?" Dwayne told Chandler what had happened. "I saw that in the paper. Where they were homeless and living in their car, right? I didn't see your name mentioned in the article."

"I asked them not to. I don't know the family at all. I wish I could have done more for them, but they were all dead by then, with the exception of the wife, and she didn't last that long after I got to them. The children were bundled up in the back seat. The husband had…he killed himself, I think when he figured out what he'd done. The missus asked me to call her sister to let her know. Brooks is trying to get the police to allow me to call her for them." Chandler asked if he could help. "I don't know. I never thought of asking you guys, but you do have an in with the station house. I just need it to get the phone number for a woman by the name of Brit. I might have heard that wrong, but I'm hoping I'm close enough to it that I can call her."

"You have it. It's Brittany Handle. She lives in New York." Chandler said that would help. "I'm going to make a call now to the station and see what they can tell me. If they'd just get you the number, that will have next of kin notified."

"Yes, that would be great. If it's all right with

the family." Chandler told him that their last name was Lance. He asked him if he wanted their names as well. "It might go a long way in convincing the other woman that I'm not a crackpot. Please. Get it for me."

Dwayne followed Chandler to Sawyer's office. His brother had been doing work with the police station for weeks now, and his office looked like a crime scene to him. He knew that pictures of the scene were helpful, but the ones on his brother's walls were bloody and vivid.

"Have you seen Gunner's office? Andi took all his medals that he no longer wore and had them framed with the information on the back as to why he received each one of them. I had no idea that Gunner was such a hero." Dwayne said he'd not seen them yet. "You need to have a look at it. It's beautifully done and very tastefully out there that he's been saving lives for a decade."

While his brother talked to someone on the phone, Dwayne had a look around this office. It was filled out nicely. He even liked the fact that there was a nice couch across from the desk rather than just chairs. Dwayne envied his brothers' tastes. Everything in this room said a man worked in here. It wasn't for show. He supposed if he ever got around to fixing his office up, he'd have a nice one too. Right now, all he had in the room was a few boxes of books, as well as an office chair.

Dwayne was working with Holly. Not for her, she told him, but with. She had not really hinted but outright told him that she was grooming him to take over her businesses when she'd had enough. Dwayne thought she was kidding. Apparently, she didn't kid around about money and how she made it.

"I knew the second I saw you that you'd make the perfect replacement for me. I bet if I were to ask you anyone around here's name today, you'd be able to tell me what it was." He said they knew who he was, so it was only fair that he learned their names. "That, right there, is what I'm talking about. You're not just a good replacement, Dwayne, but a person that I can be proud of. My son, as you know, doesn't want it. He said he's busy learning to live since that horrid wife of his was sent off to prison. Not that I blame him. Being shackled to her should have killed him. But he is being a good son and grandfather to those children."

"Molly loves him. She is having so much fun with her sister and brother that I'm surprised she ever gets out much. Raven said she's been the best big sister she could have ever hoped for." Holly told him that was the way it should be. "I agree. My parents love them too. Molly goes to their home several times a week just to hang out with them. I hope if I ever get a mate, then children, they're like her. Molly is a wonderful kid."

"I'd like to take full credit for that, but I can't. Don't tell her I said this, but I think Raven did a wonderful job of raising her on her own. I helped when she'd let me. Also, Raven doesn't have all those stupid rules that keep me from having fun with her daughter." Dwayne didn't mention her other grandmother. That was a sore spot for all of them. "Did I tell you that my son is going on a cruise with me next month? We've never done that before. I think he'll enjoy it too. While I'm gone, you'll be running the business."

"Dwayne?" He looked at his brother, being pulled from the panic attack he had every time he thought of running the business. "Here's the number. The phone doesn't have service, and I don't think it has for a long time. The captain there had to plug it in for it to come on. The battery was shot."

Taking the number from his brother, he laid it by the phone and took in a deep breath. He'd never done anything remotely like this before—called someone to let them know their family member had passed away. Chandler left him there. He also told him that he was alone in the room. Picking up the phone, he glanced at his watch as he only just realized he was happy it wasn't too late.

"Brit Handle's office. How may I help you?" He was shocked for a moment but gathered himself up quickly. Asking to speak to Brit on a personal matter got him nowhere with the person on the other end. "Do you have any idea how many men call in here thinking I'm a sap and I'm going to hand the phone over to my boss? Plenty. I like my job very much, and the person I work for. So come up with another story, or I'm hanging up."

"It's about her sister and her family." There was a long pause, and Dwayne was terrified she'd hung up on him. She told him, however, that she was Brit. "I'm sorry, Ms. Handle. But they died the day before yesterday."

"How? I'm assuming that fucktard did it." Dwayne told her how he'd found them and that her sister, while alive, didn't last long. He did ask her who fucktard was. "Her father-in-law. Howie Lane. Even his name is lazy sounding. It's his name too. Howie. I'm babbling right now, so bear with me, all right?"

"Yes, of course. Your sister's dying wish was for me to contact you." He heard a door shut, cutting off the noises that were in the background of the call. "The police usually do this, call the family, but I'd been asked to contact you, and I wanted to do that for her. If it helps you to know, it looked as if the children had simply fallen asleep and died that way. Not that having children die is a good thing. Now I'm babbling."

"It's hard to take. I mean, we weren't really all that close. You said they were in a car. Do you know if they were living anywhere?" He said they couldn't find an address for them anywhere. Also, the plates on the car had been expired for a few years. "It sounds like Howie kicked them out. Howie wanted to make his son pay for putting him in prison. I'm guessing he's finally gotten his wish."

"Howard had been shot in the head. I just assumed it was self-inflicted when I saw that he'd been shot. Do you suppose Howie had anything to do with that?" She said she didn't know but wouldn't put it past him. "The coroner has released their bodies to me. I've made arrangements to have them taken to the local funeral home. Other than prepping the bodies, there hasn't been anything done. Nothing in the paper either."

"Good. I'm going to be there in a few days. I can't leave right now because of things going on here. Isn't that the way it always is? Anyway, I have a lot going on here that requires my attention. When I get my flight information, can you arrange for us to be picked up? I'll be bringing my son with me. Is that all right?"

"Yes, of course. I can either put you up in a hotel or a bed and breakfast. Either one will be ready when you arrive. May I ask how old your son is? That way, I can figure out if he needs a crib or not." Her laughter made him smile. "I take it he won't need a crib."

"Not hardly. He's twelve going on thirty. He's the type of kid that keeps his mom straight. His name is Jamison, but he goes by Jamie. Calling him Jamison will make him roll his eyes at you. But the bed and breakfast sounds better than a hotel. Also, can you do me a favor? If you can't, then that's fine too. I'm sure you have more important things to do than help a woman out with a kid. But if you could find a local cemetery that will let them be buried there, that would be wonderful. I don't know where they were living, but they don't have anyone around here either." Dwayne was taking notes on what she wanted when she laughed. He paused in writing down calling the cemetery. "I don't even know your name. I'm so sorry."

"That's fine. It's Dwayne Bishop. My family is well known around here in the event you wanted to check us out before coming here." She asked him if he was in the habit of calling strangers to tell them that their family had died. "No. This is my first call. I just don't want you to think I'm trying to scam you."

"Mr. Bishop, I've been scammed by the best of them and have come out on top. I just want to get my sister and her family someplace where it's nice and then come back here. Dealing with Howie is going to take up a great deal of my time, but he is going to pay. I have a feeling he's the sole reason they were living out of their car." He told her he'd find out for her. "Do you have a crystal ball, by chance?"

"No. But I do have some very well connected family members. I'll see what I can find out for you before you arrive." She thanked him three times before he was able to get off the phone with her. "I'll see you in a few days, Ms. Handle."

After hanging up, he asked Sasha if she'd

help him out. When she came into the room with him, he told her what Ms. Handle had told him, as well as what he might need in the way of answers from the family.

"All right. I can do that for you. But before we go too far, Mr. Lane didn't kill himself. He wants that known so that he can be buried next to his family. I wasn't sure what he was meaning by that, but I got it figured out. Also, they think they were murdered. The mister's father had been trying to do that since they married." Dwayne asked her if she knew why. "Not yet. They're still trying to remember details about things. The little ones haven't said a word since they showed up with you. I'm thinking it's the norm for them to be quiet all the time. Also, the missus, she said to thank you for calling her sister."

"She'll be here in a few days with her son." Sasha asked him if he knew if there was a husband. "I didn't ask. Why?"

"I don't know. I was thinking she might be yours or Quincey's mate. I mean, that's the way it seems to go, don't you think?" He told her he didn't have time for a mate. "You make sure you tell her that when she arrives. All right. Ask your questions, and we'll go from there."

Chapter 1

Looking over the paperwork he'd been given last night for this meeting, Dwayne was startled when he looked up and found his dad sitting in his office. Smiling at him, he asked if he'd been there long.

"Not really. Watching you talk to yourself. What are you doing there, son?" He told him. "So you're going to meetings and making people see reason. You were always good at that as a boy too. Especially when it came to you kids having something to argue about, which was more often than not. What are you doing for lunch? Want to have some with this old man?"

"Dad, I'd love to have lunch with you." Dad lowered his head and said maybe next time. "Dad? What's going on? You don't want to have lunch now? I've not eaten, and it's well past noon."

"I thought I was going to hear a 'but' in there." Dwayne stood up and pulled his jacket off the hanger. "You sure do spiffy up well. I know all you boys look good in a suit, but you take it to a new level."

"Thanks. I'm getting so used to wearing one that I think I'm naked when I don't. By the way, you invited, but this is on me. I'm a lucky man to have lunch with my dad. We need to do this more often." Dad said he'd like that, but Dwayne could tell he had something else on his mind. Letting him think about it, the two of them walked across the street from the office building and into the steak house. "This place has the best steak sub, Dad. Mom's is better, but this one is a close second. They have pie too. Usually apple and something else."

They were seated, and Dwayne was talking about all the things he had encountered in the contract he'd been reading, knowing full well his dad wasn't really paying attention. When he finally looked up at him, Dad looked straight at him with tears streaming down his cheeks. Dwayne got up and sat in the chair next to his dad rather than across from him.

"Tell me what's happened. If I can't fix it for you, I'll get one of the others to do it." Dad shook his head and blew his nose on the large red and white handkerchief that he forever had on him. "Dad? You're scaring me. What's happened?"

"I'm useless." Dwayne just stared at his dad when he spoke. "Your mom has a job. She told me yesterday that she was loving not being at home. What's a man supposed to think when his wife says that to him? Even little Holly has a job she goes to with them babies. I'd like to say I could do that, but I'm not as energetic as I used to be. Honestly, I love them, I do, but they wear this old man out."

"First of all, stop calling yourself an old man. You're not. Secondly, have you tried finding you something that you enjoy? I know it's too late in the year for you to help with a garden, but you have that to look forward to." He said he wasn't a baby. "Sorry, Dad, but the way you're acting right now, I'm hard pressed not to be thinking that."

"That ain't even nice, son. And here I was thinking you'd be kind to me." He asked if he'd gone to one of the others. "Sawyer first—he told me to get my head out of my butt. I don't even want to tell you what Raven said. Then Quincy. He told me I was being childish too. I'm a grown man."

"Then act like it." Dwayne sat down across from him again. "I don't mean to be disrespectful to you, Dad, but you scared me to death with this. Get yourself something to do. If you want, I'm sure you can get a job just about anywhere. As you said, you're a grown man."

Their waitress came and took their order. Since his dad was in a snit now, Dwayne ordered them both steak subs and fries. Dwayne looked at his dad. He wondered if his dad knew that he looked older when he was pissed. His hair was messy and looked like he'd put his hand through it several times a minute. Dwayne thought of something he'd been meaning to talk to his dad about.

"Are you going to sit there not speaking to me, or do you want to listen to the problem I have? I don't like that you're mad at me when everyone you've spoken to, I'm betting including Mom, has told you the same thing." Dad looked at him. There was still a bit of anger there. "I would like to have a larger deck put on my house. I have one now, but it's oddly shaped. Not to mention, it seems to be too narrow to put much on it other than just a chair. Also, since there is one on the upper floor, out of the master bedroom, I'd like to see if I could get the two of them connected somehow. That way, if I'm out, I don't have to come through the house to go to my room."

"You thinking of hiring someone out for it?" Chandler had said he could do it, but Dwayne really wanted it done sooner rather than when he had the time to work on it. "I could do it. Not by my lonesome, but I could head it up. That deck being put on the back of me and your mom's new home is something I come up with. Remember working on houses when we needed some money? We all did a fine enough job that we were hired all summer for it."

"I remember that. Mrs. Miller reminded me the other day how we'd put her deck on her house in less time than she expected. She said it looks as good all these years later as it did back then. That's the kind of deck I was thinking about. Something large enough for a couple of tables spread around. Some benches. I'd like to do something like she did, too, with it butting up against the pool. The way it is now, I have to walk in the wet grass to go into the house after a good swim. Not that I'm lazy, but it would be really nice to be able to have a swim without tracking cut grass into the house."

They were still going over what he wanted in the way of a deck when their food arrived. Dad was enjoying himself. That was the point, he supposed, in him bringing it up. He could have had the deck in by now had he hired someone when he'd thought about it. But this was better. His dad was going to do it, and it would mean all that much more to them both.

"It's getting kinda cold out now. I'd be able to get the foundation down now and the rest of it in when we have a good warm day. Then in the spring, when it's warmer, I can have it stained for you. Should be able to get it in and ready before the snow hits us." He told him that would be wonderful. "This ain't no busywork, is it, son?"

"Busywork? I have no idea what that would even mean. Dad, I'm so busy all the time now that I barely have time to wash my laundry. I don't know what I'd have done if Mom hadn't sent Mrs. Crowe over to cook and clean up after me." Dwayne laughed. "The other day, she saved me by having my laundry coming out of the dryer just as I was running down the stairs to go to work. She's a marvel."

"I sure do like having people cleaning up after me too. I know the house we're gonna be moving into is bigger and new, but still, knowing that when you put something in the laundry basket, it's going to be washed up right away is really wonderful." Dad laughed a little nervously as he looked around the restaurant. "Don't be telling your mom what I said. She'll have my hide on that."

His dad left him in a much better mood. Dwayne did reach out to his brothers and told them what Dad was up to. They all agreed he did need a job—at least something to do that would keep him busy. Dad tended to get into all kinds of hot water when he was bored. Dwayne personally thought he got himself into trouble because he got the attention he wanted. Good or bad, someone was talking to him.

The little boy was coming around the corner at a quick pace and knocked into Dwayne. As soon as he put this hands on the kid to keep him from falling, he looked up at him. His lip was bloody, his nose was bleeding, and it looked as if he was going to have a shiner in a few hours. Shoving him behind him when the Sharon boys came around the same building, Dwayne asked them what they were up to.

"Nothing, Mr. Bishop." One of the kids looked around him. "We was playing with Jamie there, and he pussyed out on us. That's not the way to play football. We were thinking on showing him some more moves."

The kid behind him, Jamie, he assumed, put his hand into his. Dwayne could feel the scrapes there as well. Holland Sharon, he thought the oldest boy was, reached for Jamie and pulled him out from behind him.

"Stop." No one moved. Not only that, but Holland released Jamie too. "Now, why don't you tell me what really happened? That way, I don't have to call my mom here to ask you. She's right across the street in her shop if you guys wouldn't mind going—"

"They were not showing me how to play. The oldest one there, Holland, came at me when I was just walking down the street. My mom is going to be so mad when she sees what I look like." It was then Dwayne noticed that all three of the Sharon boys were sporting bumps and bruises as well. "I was winning that fight, too, when they hit me in the face with a ball bat."

"You took all three of them on? And only have a black eye to show for it? Good for you." He turned to the Sharon boys again. "It's bad enough that you beat each other up, but you also take on one kid that is new to town. Then if that's not enough, when he's winning the fight, you play dirty. Christ, your mom is going to have a cow when I tell her."

"You're going to tell on us? We was just having a bit of fun." Looking at Jamie, then back at Holland, Dwayne shrugged. It was then that Holland's voice turned hard and mean. "Well, I didn't say he was having any fun. I guess we're going to be in trouble again, and it'll be all his fault. I'm going to get you, kid."

Running them off, he could see that Holland was going to get Jamie the next time he saw him. And he'd bet anything it would be nothing but vicious for what he thought was retaliation. He turned to look at Jamie.

"I don't know you, do I?" He said he was there with his mom to settle up things with his aunt and uncle. "The Lane family, I take it."

"Yes. She was just going to be here a couple of days, but then they figured out that they'd been murdered by Mr. Lane. Uncle Howard's dad. Can I come in there with you? I need to call my mom. She's going to have a fit. Not that I was defending myself, she'd be all right with that, but because I bothered you. And my clothes. Sheesh, she just got me this shirt, too."

Careful not to laugh at Jamie, he took him inside the Addington building with him. Jamie had his picture taken for his badge, as well as his thumbprint, so he'd have access to any part of the building from now on. The latter wasn't necessary, but Jamie was having such a good time that no one could turn him down. As soon as they were in Dwayne's office, he asked if Jamie wanted to call his mom.

"Yes, sir. Just so you know, my mom is a ball buster. I don't call her that to her face, but that's what everyone calls her." Dwayne asked him who told him that. "She did. Mom thinks it's funny. I had to ask her what it meant. That's not a nice thing, do you think, Mr. Bishop?"

"I don't know that it's a bad thing either. I mean, I have four sisters-in-law that are the same way. They think someone is complimenting them when they get called that. I just try and stay out of their way." Jamie said he did as well when his mom was in one of her moods. "Yes, that's a good idea. Perhaps you're a good deal smarter than I first thought."

When Jamie asked to use the bathroom, Dwayne told him he could use his. When he came out, his face and hands washed, he didn't look any better. Also, he thought a few of the places he'd been hit were making themselves known to him.

"Mr. Bishop, I don't feel so good." Dwayne was halfway out of his chair when Jamie fell backward. There was blood on his hand when he picked him up from the floor, and he turned the little guy over.

"Christ." Calling out to his secretary, he told her to call an ambulance. "Call my mom too. Have her get in touch with Jamie's mother. I don't know her, but Mom does." He looked back at Jamie. "Come on, kid. You're going to be all right. Come on now. Open your eyes for me."

He didn't. By the time the medics were in his office, Dwayne had called his brother Quincey and told him what he'd found. Dwayne had never been so afraid in his life as he was just then. It had never occurred to him to have a look at him when they'd been together. Now the kid was going to be scarred for life.

Jamie finally opened his eyes to look at him, but only long enough to empty his belly all over the team with him. This was bad, he told himself. Really bad.

~*~

Brit was both glad and pissed off that no

one would let her drive. Sawyer was going fast, she'd give him that, but he wasn't going fast enough for her heart. Her little boy was hurting, and she wasn't there for him.

"I've spoken to my brother. Dwayne said it looked to him like he'd hit his head hard on something." He then told her about the Sharon boys. "I'm going to drop you off at the hospital, then I'm going to go and have a talk with them. More than likely, bring them in. Not that we've had this sort of serious trouble from them before, but they're not good kids. Will you press charges?"

"I can't think beyond wanting them to be dead right now. I know that's harsh, but Jamie has had all kinds of self-defense classes, and if these kids got the better of him, then it must be bad." Sawyer explained again what he knew about his head injury. "I know. It looks bad. I'm to understand he's said that to you a couple of hundred times. Please don't say it to me again. My mind is all over the place with what bad looks like to your brother. I'm hoping he's just a little freaked out, and it won't be that bad."

"All right." He was nearly to the hospital when he turned to her again. "My brother Quincey is there now. He said that Jamie will be having a CAT scan when you arrive. He couldn't wait, as he wanted to be sure there is nothing permanently wrong with him."

"He thinks it's bad too." Sawyer didn't say anything as he was driving into the emergency lane that would put her in front of the department. "How is my son, Sawyer? Honestly."

"Quincey said he'll be fine if there is nothing more pressing with his head. There will be a great many stitches. He'll have to rest for a while and more than likely have to spend a couple of days in the hospital. I want you to also know that my brother Dwayne, who was with Jamie when he passed out, is beyond stressed. So if you could, would you please cut him some slack? He might explode on you. Not talk to you badly, but have a breakdown. He's that close, Quincey said." She told him she would try very hard not to say anything stressful to him. "Thank you. Dwayne is a good man, but he doesn't like it when children suffer. It hurts him deep in his heart, he told me once."

Getting out of the car then, she made her way into the emergency department. In a passing sort of way, she noticed that everything was nice in the department. Planters full of flowers. There were pictures around the room that she'd bet were taken around the area. When she saw Mrs. Bishop, she grabbed onto her like a lifeline.

"They've taken him up to get some pictures of his head. Poor little lamb. All he talked about was you coming here and that I was to stick with you." She asked if he was talking a lot. "To me, it seemed like a great deal what with his injuries. You'll be happy to know that Quincey was pleased that he not only knew his name but his birthday and what year it is. Also that you two were only here for a few more days, coming from New York. All good signs."

Glancing up from her chair, Brit saw the young man coming toward them. He had blood on his shirt as well as his pants. Brit knew right away that it was Dwayne. When he asked her if she was Jamie's mom, she told him she was. Then, before he could tell her anything more, she put up her hand and spoke first.

"Thank you for saving him. I've no doubt at all that Jamie was trying his best to be brave around you, and that is what made him faint. Also, thank you so much for protecting him from those boys. Your brother, Sawyer, told me he was headed there to talk to them now." He asked her if she was going to press charges. "I might not have if Sawyer hadn't told me they weren't good kids in the first place. They could have killed anyone with their meanness. Thank you for that."

"He didn't run to me so much as he ran into me." Dwayne sat down. "I didn't see anything beyond he had a busted lip and a blackening eye. The other three looked a great deal more beat up. I shouldn't have done it, but I praised Jamie for taking on three and coming out ahead until the ball-bat was brought into play."

"I would have too had he come to me." Dwayne looked at her. "What? I can't be proud of him for coming out almost on top in a very uneven fight? What else did he tell you?"

"Why the two of you were here. Also that you were going to be mad because you'd only just gotten him the shirt he had on. They cut it off him before we got here." Brit thanked him again for taking care of her son. "There are a couple of things he had in his pocket when they brought him in. Since the entire town knows us, they turned it over to me. I hope that is all right with you."

He stood for a few seconds as he dug for whatever it was he had in his pocket. When he put it into her hand, the jolt to her system nearly knocked her off the chair she was sitting on. Brit knew what it meant just a few seconds before Dwayne did.

"No. I mean, hell no." Dwayne didn't say anything, but he did look at his mother when she asked him what had happened. "He's going to try and be my mate. I don't think so. I have my life just where I want it after one failed marriage. I'm not going to go through that shit again just because someone's DNA has figured that I need to be someone to pamper him."

"Are you finished?" She turned and looked at Dwayne. "I mean, if you have more to say on the subject, then go on and get it out of your system. I understand you're stressed, and I am as well. However, I want you to remember this. I'm not whoever that was before. Not even close. I'm just as surprised by it as you are. But you'll notice I didn't fly off the handle and start accusing you of anything." He stood up. "Mom, I'm going back to my office. I have a great deal of paperwork I have to finish up for tomorrow. If you'd not mind, Mom, could you let me know about Jamie? I'd really appreciate it."

He left. Just left them there after kissing his mom on her cheek. Brit turned to Sippy and told her she was sorry. Instead of telling her, it was all right, she just turned back in her seat.

"One of the other girls did that to one of my sons. I vowed then that I'd not get into it with them if one of you women were to do that again. So I won't tell you how you're barking up the wrong tree with my son. Nor will I point out that he'd not said a single word to you before you blasted him." She finally looked at her. "I've just heard from my other son, the one that has been caring for your son since he arrived, and he said Jamie is being put into a room to spend a couple of nights here until they get tests back. I'd really appreciate it if you were to cool your jets."

"Yes, ma'am."

They went to the fifth floor without saying a word. Sippy was greeted happily by the women at the desk. Brit felt like all kinds of a fool when she was introduced to the women as Dwayne's mate. Asking what room her boy was in, she was told, and Brit made her way there. Barely making it before she started crying, she found the room empty except for the two chairs in the room. Taking one, she sat down and cried harder than she had in some time.

Not wanting Jamie to find her upset, she went to the bathroom and freshened herself up. Her eyes were red, but she could blame that on stress. When she came out of the bathroom, Sippy was sitting in one of the chairs, so she took the other. The silence was very heavy in the room.

Looking out the window, down at the snow just coming down and covering the cars in the parking lot, Brit was crying again when Jamie was brought into the room, and he reached for her.

"I'm so sorry, Mom. I know you're stressed out enough." He looked around. "Hello, Mrs. Sippy. I thought Dwayne would be here. He's been really nice since they brought me in here."

"He's gone back to work. Something about a big project he's working on. But he did want me to leave his cell phone number for you to call him when you have the time."

Who Brit thought was Quincey came into the room then. He kissed his mother and then looked at Brit.

"We've looked at the CAT scan, and it doesn't look as if he has any breaks or cracks in his skull. But we'll have a radiologist have a look at them soon. I have put seventy-five stitches in his head that will have to be watched carefully. Also, he does have a couple of busted ribs that I believe will heal on their own. The black eye is fine as well. No damage to his eye or his eyeball that causes me any concern. There are also five stitches in his lower lip that he'll be able to tell women about when he's older. Do you have any questions?" She asked when they could go back home. "I'd not make any plans for a few days at least. Also, Sawyer said you were pressing charges against the Sharon boys. That's a good idea. Jamie will need quiet while he's recuperating. And I'd not recommend him flying. The compression in a plane at this point would give him a headache beyond anything he's ever had before."

"I had one now. Doctor Quincey gave me some happy juice, he called it. I don't hurt one bit." He giggled, and she laughed too. "I think that whatever it is, Mom, you should get some when you're upset. It takes all the stress away too."

Jamie snuggled up to her hand and promptly fell asleep. When she looked at Quincey again, he sat down in the chair his mom had been in. Brit felt ashamed that she'd not even noticed Sippy had left already. She asked Quincey if he was going to lecture her. Not that she didn't deserve it, but she asked if he could wait.

"No. No lectures from me. I heard, of course, that you and Dwayne are mates. And that you were upset about it. I don't know how much you know about cat mates, but you can ask if you wish more information." She told him for now, she wanted to focus on her son. "Understandable. As I said, he'll need quiet. When the pain medication wears off, he's going to be in a great deal of pain. Encourage him to take the medication before the pain gets the better of him. He's a great kid, but I think you've told him about pain medication and how easy it is to get addicted to it. Good for you. However, the little we're giving him will be all right until his head heals a little. There isn't any point in him being in pain when it's not necessary."

"I'll do that. Thank you." When she didn't have anything more to ask, he left her there. Looking at Jamie, all she had in the world, Brit let the tears fall as much as they wanted. Her son was hurt, and she'd hurt other people too. It wasn't in her to be so cruel or mean when it wasn't warranted.

Waking up when a nurse asked her if she needed anything, she looked at Jamie. "He's been sleeping well. I've given him a little more pain medication when he could have it, so he'll continue to rest. Doc Quincey said you'd be all right with that."

"Yes. He needs to rest more, he told me."

She smiled at her and told her he was doing fine. "I've not had anything to eat for a while. Is there a cafeteria around? I won't be gone but a few minutes."

"Dwayne had something to eat sent over for you. Hang on while I get it for you." Her guilt was getting heavier all the time. When the nurse returned, she had not just a bag of food for her but two bottles of water as well. "It's a sample box of subs. He didn't know what you liked, so he had them make you up some that you might try. You can't go wrong with those, Ms. Handle. Those are the best there is. He sent us some of them too. Nicest men, those Bishop men."

And the guilt trip was getting better and better, she thought. Not that it was Dwayne's fault that she was a bitch. She was, and she knew it. But all he'd done was take care that not only did her son get medical help but that she was notified as well. Sitting back in her chair, she wondered how she'd go about getting in touch with him. Groveling was the only way she was going to fix this. Brit ate one of the subs while she thought about what she'd say to him. Or to anyone in his family to get the number.

While sitting there contemplating if she wanted another sub, she saw the receipt. It had his first name on it, as well as his phone number. Or at least she hoped it was his number. There was no amount on it, but the name of the place was a place she'd passed a couple of times on her way around town. Eating the second sub simply because it was that good, she made herself notes on what she wanted to say to him on the paper bag her food had come in. Before she got too far along, the man she was thinking about showed up in the doorway.

"My mom sent me over to check on Jamie." She asked him to have a seat. "I don't mean to intrude, Ms. Handle. I only came by to check on him for my family."

"Please. I'm so sorry. Will you please have a seat so I can grovel? I was just getting ready to call you when you showed up." She showed him the receipt that had his phone number on it. "Is this how I get in touch with you?"

"That's my office phone. I don't usually answer it, but it's there, so I use that instead of my— I didn't do anything to you. You're aware of that, aren't you? I was as shocked as you were when we touched."

"Mom?"

Crying again, sobbing really, she held onto her son while he held her. Dwayne didn't leave them after Jamie asked him to stay. All she could do was hold onto Jamie and beg for forgiveness from a very nice man.

Chapter 2

"There are only two options in dealing with this sort of product, Mr. Shelby. One is that you find a market that can afford it. While I think there might be a couple of hundred people in this state alone that will be able to do that, the second thing is trickier. Once they buy your device, there isn't a reason at all to purchase anything else. Everything anyone ever wants to record on it can be purchased or even downloaded from the Internet." Mr. Shelby told him that wasn't the way he wanted it to be used. "Regardless, they will. Having a player that only plays the music you wish for them to purchase is going to limit you to who will enjoy the music and podcasts you're hoping to sell as extras. That alone will make people more pissed off about the product in that you're making decisions based on your likes and dislikes. It won't work that way. Something else you will want to consider, you're only catering to older people that might not have a cell phone that can do the same thing for a great deal less money. Once that demographic is gone, there will be no one left that will care to have a playlist several thousand songs long."

"I've been working on this for years, Mr. Bishop. What am I supposed to do now that I'm not going to make any money on it? It's all I know." Dwayne sat down. Keeping his mouth shut was difficult, but he knew Mr. Shelby had to work this out on his own. "My granddaughter, Linsey, she told me she loves hers. How are you so sure everyone won't love it?"

"Did she pay you for hers?" He looked indignant. "I'll take that as a no. That is the reason. Also, she's your granddaughter. Have you thought perhaps she might be telling you that because you thought enough of her to let her try it out? I know I do that with my parents. Not much, mind you, but I do. I'm not going to be able to lend you the money, sir. Not for this. However, I have been working on a list of things you could do for income. And they're right up your alley."

He handed the list over to the man across from him just as his mom contacted him. *I know you're very busy, but I wanted to let you know that Jamie is going home in the morning. I'm sure you would have found that out when you went by there, but I wanted to give you some good news.* Dwayne felt the relief all the way to his toes. *He and his mom are coming over for dinner as soon as it can be arranged. When that's fixed up, all of you are to be here. We're having a roast and all the trimmings. Make sure you can make it, all right? Oh, and we're having dinner with her tonight as well, just to get everybody together and calm things down.*

I will be there. He wanted to ask her more about Jamie, but Mr. Shelby started talking. *I have to go, Mom. I'll see you tonight.*

"These are just repair jobs. I'm better than that." Instead of pointing out that he wasn't in the market to be picky about things, Dwayne slid another paper to the man. "Where did you get this? Are you trying to make me do something I don't want to just so you can have me give up on my dreams? It won't work."

"I'd never crush someone's dreams. That's not how we work here anyway. However, those are prices that people are charging right now to repair someone's CD player. There are a great many people that are die-hard purists when it comes to their music. If you'll look, that company there is getting nearly five hundred dollars just to fix people's turntables. Even to replace a needle on it could cost upwards of a hundred dollars. The one I think would work best for you is the speaker repairs. I've seen your warehouse. You could do that right now, and it wouldn't be something you'd have to wait on product to do."

"I do have a lot of the material I can use now. I collect stuff when I can get it cheap." He looked over the page and then looked at Dwayne. "Could I do this with your funding and use my profits from repairing speakers, when I get them, to pay you back?"

"So long as you understand, anything you use the money for other than to repair speakers is going to null and void our contract, and you'll be responsible for paying it all back plus interest. I don't think you'll do that—you're not a stupid man—but I want to put that out there for you to remember." He nodded, looking at the paper again. "Mr. Shelby, I know a woman that works in the television movie media that is forever looking for older pieces of things to rent for movie productions. They use the things when they're doing a period piece. I can see you working with her or even selling what you have to her for her to rent out too. I'm not entirely sure how that would work—I've not a lot of information on it—but I'm betting she is in the market for stereo equipment. If she's not, then perhaps she can hook you up with someone that might be able to use it."

"You'd do that for me? Even though you turned me down on the player project?" He said he wanted them both to make some money. "Yes, I can see that. Mrs. Addington, she sure did do it up right when she hired you, young man. I'm going to tell her when I see her, too. You're a good man."

"Thank you."

After Mr. Shelby left, asking for a couple of days to figure things out on what he wanted to do, Dwayne pulled the next file to him just as his secretary came into the office with him. She put a bottle of water on his desk, along with his messages. The one on the top was from Brit.

"She's called here a couple of times today. I thought she was a crackpot, telling me that she was your mate. But then, when your mom called, I took her more seriously. You should have given me her name, and I would have put her through to you." He said he wasn't sure she'd ever have a reason to call him here. "Apparently, she figured out something. Brit, her name she said, made sure I knew it wasn't an emergency, but she did want to talk to you. The second time she called, she sounded overwhelmed. I don't know why—she didn't tell me—but I'd call her now if I were you. Also, did you remember I'm leaving at one today?"

"I didn't, but I have it on my calendar. Good luck with your adoption interview. Why don't you go now and get ready? I have this." She asked him if he was sure. "I am. You've already done so much for me today that you deserve it."

Picking up the phone, he called the number on the slip. He'd been talking to Brit off and on for the past couple of days. Dwayne had been careful not to mention that they were mates.

As soon as she answered, he regretted sending Mare home. "What's the matter?" Brit wasn't upset so much as she sounded like she was pissed off. He covered his mouth to not laugh out loud when she started stringing curse words together like she had a thesaurus she was getting them from. "Slow down, please. I'm getting some of it, but not enough to understand what it is you need me to do."

"I'm at your house. You asked me to go by

there, and I have. However, I did not expect for there to be a lion on the front deck nor a large fucking panther in the living room. What the hell is this place? A zoo?" He laughed then. "I don't think this is the least bit— Dwayne, the lion just laid his head on my lap, and it's freaking me out."

"Have you met Molly?" She said she had. "Good. I'm betting she's not too far. If you could call out to her, she can get the lion and the panther out of the house. I didn't know they'd come into the house, but they're harmless."

"Harmless? Are you kidding me? Have you seen their teeth?" He told her his were much larger. "Not helping, you moron. Not at all." She yelled for Molly, and he heard the moment she was coming to Brit's rescue.

"The lion is a friend of Molly's. His name is Shed. I know it's hard to believe right now, but he's very gentle. Also, the panther isn't a he but a she, and she comes into the house through the doggie door that was there before I got the house. She's going to have kittens, and she lies in the living room because she can stretch out and be warm. Is Molly helping you?" Brit told him she was. "Good. Okay, she'll get them out of the way for you. They live on Gunner's property with a few other cats. They won't hurt you at all so long as you're not being aggressive to anyone."

"Can I expect this all the time? Cats roaming the house like they own it?" He said he'd remove the doggie door when he got home. "No, don't do that. I'm sorry I freaked out. I've just never— He licked me."

"He did that to get your scent. I don't know if he can understand you or not, but will you have Molly tell him that you're my mate? That way, he'll not bother you when you come around. As I said, he and Molly are good friends." When she seemed less stressed, he asked her about going to his parents' house for dinner. "Mom let me know a little while ago. We're also doing something special when Jamie is released. I could be finished up here at five if nothing else gets in the way. I don't know that it will, but I'm forever hopeful of getting home on time."

"I'm all right now. When I first arrived, I didn't see Shed. I don't know how I missed him, but apparently, I'm not as situationally aware as I think I should be." She laughed a little. "Before I forget to tell you, Jamie wants to know if you'll come by and see him. He has a couple of questions to ask of you about this mate thing. I don't know everything he wanted to know, so I told him I'd ask you to go by."

"Yes, I can do that. No problem." He opened the file up and glanced down at it. "Oh, before I forget. Mr. Shelby was a client of mine I had today."

After telling her what the man was doing and what he'd told him, she asked him questions about his equipment. She seemed really excited and asked if she could call him. After giving her the phone number, he asked her if that was all right.

"Yes. Very much so. If he doesn't mind traveling, I have a few pieces that need some repair work on them too. Directors love it when the things work the way they should for them. If he'd not mind, I can keep him working if he can look over some other things I have." He told her what the man wanted to do. "I have a few CD players as well. Neither of them works. Yes, I'll call him. This will be great for both of us."

After telling her he'd go see Jamie, he got back to work. When his alarm went off at twelve-thirty, he stood up to stretch. Dwayne answered his phone just as he was headed out the door to take a walk around the upper floor. It was Holly.

"Just the man I needed to talk to. Mr. Shelby called me. My goodness, you've made an impression on him. And I'm so happy you gave him options on what he could do." He told her what Brit had told him. "Brilliant. Just brilliant. Oh, I do hope this will work out for both of them. My goodness, I never thought of a market for things for movie sets. I haven't any idea why, but I didn't think about that. Darn it. Now I can't get into that too. But it's just as well, I think. Now I can focus on other things. I know that Mare is gone for the day. Put the phone on service and come meet me at the hospital. I've been talking with that young man Jamie, and he is a hoot. I have a few things for him as well. Did you know he'll be my great-grandson too? That's so good of you to find a mate with a little boy."

"I'm so happy I could accommodate you." She laughed, and he joined her. "I would love to meet you at the hospital. I was going to pick him up something to eat while I'm on my way. Did you want anything? I found out he's going home tomorrow, so that'll be good. He wants to speak to me about shifter things. I told his mom I'd be there for him."

"Of course you will. No, no. I've eaten too much for lunch as it is. All right. I'll meet you in the lobby in about twenty minutes. I might be a tad late, Dwayne. Knowing he'll be going home tomorrow just gave me an idea on what else he'll need." He reminded her that he wasn't his son just yet. "Pee shaw, Dwayne. You know as well as I do that you're going to win her heart. I'm betting you already have the young man's. I'll meet you in the lobby. Love you, kiddo."

He transferred the phone over to the service and went downstairs to head over to get him something to eat. Holly was rarely on time. And since she'd warned him that she was headed to a store, he knew he'd be lucky if she was only an hour behind. Picking up some food for him and Jamie to have, he also picked up some turnovers. Cherry for Jamie and blueberry for himself. Also, picking up a cheese Danish, he took it with him when he paid so that Holly would have something to enjoy as well.

It was almost an hour after the twenty minutes she said she'd need. When he got into the limo with her, he didn't mention it or the five bags of things between them. Dwayne did tell her about the Danish he'd gotten for her, and she kissed him on the cheek.

"What do you know about this young woman?" He told her nothing more than she'd let him know. "She's had a hard life, Dwayne. Brooks was telling me she not only had a hard time of it as a child but that her husband was a druggy as well as an abusive bastard. Could be why she was so upset with you in the first place."

"You heard about that, did you? Well, don't tell me anything else. When she's ready to tell me, I guess she will." Holly patted him on the cheek and told him he was a good boy. "I hope she thinks I'm more than a boy, Holly. I could be in big trouble if she thinks of me that way."

When they pulled into the parking lot at the hospital, the driver helped her take her purchases in. Dwayne had a few of them in his hand as well, and he was pleased to see Jamie sitting in a chair when they arrived. He even looked better, he thought.

"Wow, this is all for me?" Holly told him that if he was going to be her grandchild, he should have the most up to date things. "Mom will have a cow, but I thank you very much. Is that a sub, Mr. Dwayne? I'm starving to death."

"Good. My mom would say you're on the mend." He took the sub and fries and left the bags and packages on the bed. "I've been thinking of one of these all day. The lunch they brought me wasn't good. I'm not saying that because it wasn't what I wanted, but it wasn't good. Even the nurse told me it smelled bad. But this is the best."

The two of them ate while Holly opened some of the bags she'd brought in. Not only had she gotten him a reader, but she'd gotten him a laptop as well. As soon as he finished eating, which seemed to perk him up a bit more, he looked over the things she'd gotten him. The kid was the politest kid he'd ever met—besides Molly and the other children in the family. They were perfect too.

~*~

"Hello, Jamie." Jamie smiled at Doc Quincey. "I see you've been getting up and around well. That's really good news for both of us. I have an idea to let you go home today. How about that?"

"Seriously? I'd love it. My mom will be so happy too." Dwayne asked if he could take him home to surprise her. "Yes, that would be perfect. She will be so happy. If I know my mom, she won't sleep a wink tonight worrying about me coming home tomorrow."

Jamie tried very hard not to be overly excited. It gave him pains in his head, something terrible. Once they had all his things packed up, Ms. Holly told him she'd take him there in style. He told her how he'd never been in a limo before coming here.

"We'll have to fix that too. A young man such as yourself should be riding around in a limo all the time. You two talk and I'll go and make arrangements to have this all sent over to Dwayne's home. Is that where you and your mother are staying?" He looked at Dwayne, and when he nodded, it was all he could do not to leap for joy. "All right. I'll be back in a bit now. Quincey said he'd have the paperwork fixed up for you in about a half-hour. I'll be back before then."

When the door shut behind her, Dwayne laughed. "No, she won't. I love her like my own grandmother, but she is the most distractable person I've ever known. Don't be surprised if she adds a few more things to your gifts." They both laughed as they ate their turnovers. "What is it you wanted to talk to me about?"

"My mom. And me, I guess. But Mom mostly. She is a wonderful mom. A lot better than most of the other kids I go to school with have. But my dad, Herman, he wasn't all that nice. He knocked us around a lot. Mostly Mom, but he'd hit me too when I was too close." Dwayne asked him if he was still around. "Nah, he's dead. He held me and her hostage one day, and they had to kill him before he did Mom."

"I'm sorry about that, Jamie. I truly am. But is it all right that you tell me this?" He said it was. He'd asked his mom. "Okay then. What else? I'm sure that's not what you wanted to talk to me about."

"It's not." He played with the crumbs from his turnover before speaking again. "They weren't married. Not ever. But Mom thought it was easier, she told me, to tell people they were. Not that it excused him from hurting us, but she didn't want people to think she was a horrible person for letting him into her home."

"I can understand that. I plan on marrying your mom when she'll let me. Also, if it's all right with the two of you, I'd very much like to adopt you." Jamie glanced up at Dwayne, hope rising in his heart. "What is it you're not telling me, son? I'm feeling like there is something important you need to—"

"He raped me." After getting it out of his mouth, it was easier to tell Dwayne all of it. "I was little when he did it the first time. I didn't tell my mom until later after he hurt me so bad I couldn't go to the bathroom. That was what the police came to get him for. She filed charges against him. She'd done it before, a lot of times, but he didn't like that she was doing it, and he'd beat her worse. When he hurt us that last time, beating Mom almost to death and then hurting me too, I called the police to the house. They said they'd not come there on a domestic call again, so I called the FBI. The police weren't helping us, so I sort of went over their heads."

"Good for you." Jamie asked him if he was mad at him. "For saving your mother? Never. I think you're very brave for what you did. You more than likely saved both your lives. For me."

"You won't hurt her, will you, Dwayne? Or me?" Dwayne hugged him then. It was a little hard to let him do that until Dwayne told him he'd never hurt him. Not for all the money in the world. "My mom is so wonderful, and it hurt me so bad when she was hurt all the time. It was all I could do not to kill him myself. I think I could have done it too. I hated him that much."

"I'm proud of you, Jamie. So proud that you were smart enough to know you had to do something the police wouldn't. Also that you didn't kill Herman. That would have been ten times worse if you'd done that. Especially since you'd figured out the police weren't helping you at all." He let him go but didn't leave his side. "As I said, you won't have to worry about anyone in my family harming you in any way. Ever. My mom would box our ears if we even thought about it. I'd die for you if it came to that. I swear to you, anyone in my family would do the same. We feel that strongly about keeping the two of you safe."

Thanking him over and over, Jamie asked him about shifters. How the mate thing worked. He also asked him about what he thought of him calling his family by their given names rather than mister and missus all the time.

"My mom would be as happy as a clam if you were to call her Grandma. Holly too, but she goes by GGMa with Molly. She'd be your great-grandma. Not by blood, but she'd never think of you as anything but her great-grandchild. My family, either. So far as they'll be concerned, you'll be Jamie Bishop to them and their nephew." He asked about his dad. "My dad is already ready to bust his buttons off his shirt. He's been telling anyone that would stand still for a few minutes that you took on three boys, the Sharon boys, and came out on top, except for the ball bat. But he said they tricked you with that."

Jamie laughed. "I love your family too. Grandma brought me in a blanket yesterday. She said I needed something of my own to sleep under. She told me that she had made it." Dwayne looked at it and showed him where she'd put her name and the year on the trimmings. "That blanket is older than dirt, Grandpa told me. I love it. It smells like your mom too. All soft and sweet."

"You should tell her that if you've not already." He said he thought it was sappy. "That's all right. My mom loves it when someone gets a little sappy with her. And if you were to pick her some flowers out in the woods and take them to her, she'd be in heaven. Moms are like that, I think."

"Not my mom. She'd scold me for not allowing someone else enjoy the flowers I brought her. She'd still love them and smell them every ten minutes, but she loves plants. Of all kinds. We don't have any at our apartment in New York, but she has them in her office." He asked him why not their apartment. "We have a bastard, Mom calls him, for a landlord. He won't allow me to have any pets either. Not even a fish. He said that if the tank or planter were to spring a leak, he'd be flooded out downstairs. I don't know how much water he thinks a plant needs, but we don't have them."

Dwayne laughed with him. When

Holly returned, he'd had all, but one question answered. Jamie wasn't entirely sure how to ask—it was sort of a personal question—but he would save it for later. After spending the last few hours with him, Jamie certainly felt better about him and his mom living with Dwayne. He didn't lose his temper at all for any reason. That made him feel really good.

After being loaded up in the car, he leaned on Dwayne and covered up with his blanket. Quincey had given him something lite for the pain so he'd not hurt that much in the car, and it had worked. By the time they were pulling up in front of the big house, he was sure he'd been taken to another hotel. Turned out it was Raven and Sawyer's home.

Dwayne carried him into the house. The medication was making him a little woozy. When he was sat on the big soft couch, he saw his mom coming into the room. When she started crying, so happy, she told him that he was home, he did too. Everyone, including Dwayne, left them alone.

"I'm so happy you're here. How are you feeling?" He told her that Dwayne had his instructions. "Then I'll get them later. Are you feeling all right, honey? You look amazing. I'm sorry I couldn't come to see you today, but this is so much better. How are you feeling?"

"Mom." She smiled at him. "I feel fine. I promise I do. Dwayne and I had a nice talk, and I like him very much. He's a good man."

"I think he is as well. I was rude to him the first time I met him. I hope he doesn't hold that against me." Jamie told her he doubted he ever would. "I don't think so either, but I get nervous about things like this."

"I got to talk to him. I told him about Herman and what he did to me." She kissed him on the forehead and asked him what Dwayne had said. "He told me how proud he was of me for getting the two of us help and that he was really happy I didn't kill him. No one ever told me that before but you. Dwayne isn't even related to me yet, and he was really proud of me. Are you going to marry him?"

"He's not asked. Not that I'm ready for that yet, but we'll get to that when the timing is better." She cuddled him next to her. "There are a lot of things we have to talk about, Jamie. Like, I have a business in New York. My contacts are there. Also, we have a place there that we're going to be renting for the next two years. That's a lot of money to be paying someone if we break our contract and he sues us for it."

"I know." He watched the backyard for a moment, then sat up higher on the couch. "That's a lion. A big lion, Mom."

"Yes, we've met. His name is Shed." Jamie looked at his mom, who was so calm about meeting the big lion. "He licked my face, Jamie. All over it. I was sure he was going to eat my head, but he needed to get my scent. I think there is a panther back there as well."

"Who are you, and what did you do with my mom? You sound like it's just a natural thing for you to be licked by a lion." She said she'd been terrified at first, but then Molly helped her. "Can I meet him too? I mean—wow, a lion. I also want to see Dwayne's cat. He told me that he's white."

"I've not seen him yet. But Sawyer was out in the yard when we got here. I don't know if he's still out there, but would you like to see him if he is?" Jamie thought his mom was off her rocker. Either that, or she was taking something to have her so calm. Then she wanted him to go out into the yard with a lion? "You're shocked at me, aren't you?"

"No, whatever gave you that idea?" She laughed with him. "Can I go out, really? I've never even had a kitten to pet. This will be epic, Mom."

"Let me go and see if someone is around that can take you out. I know you can walk now, Quincey told me, but you need to keep calm, and that includes you not getting overly excited about meeting a wild beast."

While she was gone, he thought about his mom. Sheesh, being here sure did make her calmer than he'd ever seen her.

When she returned, she had Andi with her. She was a witch. He knew that. So when she just popped him into the backyard in a chair, he was laughing so hard he almost missed Shed coming to see him. He laid his big head on his lap as soon as Jamie said it was all right.

"Hello, boy. My goodness, you're beautiful." He scratched him behind the ears. Shed closed his eyes like he was going to take a nap. "You have a lot of scars on your face, don't you, boy? I hope you weren't too hurt. I'd hate that for you."

"He was a circus animal for a while. Before that, he was a leader of a large leap in Africa. My name is Molly. My mom is Raven." He told her he'd heard about her and the lion being her friend. "He's teaching me how to use my magic.

Also, how to defend myself against someone trying to hurt me."

"I took some self-defense classes in New York." He looked at Shed again. "I don't think my lessons and yours are the same, do you?"

They sat in the yard for nearly an hour. After they were called into the house to get warm, Andi popped him and Molly both into the house. Jamie could have spent the rest of his life in this place and never be bored. It was that kind of home, he thought, where anyone would be welcome.

Chapter 3

Howie read the paper every day, and there hadn't been a single thing about his son. That wasn't right. The boy was his son, and he should have at least had a little bit of the news about his demise there someplace. He was just getting his meal set in front of him when a man and a woman sat down across from him.

The man took his soup and started eating it. The woman asked for a cup of hot tea and for them to put it on his bill. When Howie reached for the soup, the man's hand came down on his and changed into a furry paw. The claws were digging deep into his hand as the man asked the woman if she wanted to start, as he was enjoying the soup.

"What gives you the right to come in here

and take a man's food from him? Then to hurt me like you are?" The claws dug deeper, and he cried out. "I'm going to call the cops on you. You see if I don't."

The man laid a gun on the table, along with a badge. Howie felt his balls tighten up around his throat. He liked to brag that he had it in good with his fellow officers, but if given the chance, any one of them, or maybe even all of them, would shoot him where he stood. Not only would they be justified for it, but he looked for it to happen every day.

The man finished his soup. "You're dirty. Not only are you dirty, but somehow you've managed to not be in prison, Howie. Really, does a grown man liked to be called Howie? Whatever floats your boat, I guess."

Another couple came into the restaurant. He would have left then, but he was blocked. Cock blocked, he thought this might be called.

"Hello, Howie. How's it hanging? Not very well, I'm betting." The new woman put up her fingers to show that he was less than half an inch after pushing her way into the booth on his side. "From what I've heard, you're not only a pencil dick, but it's just a nubbin too."

Doubling up his fist, he was hurting to

smash it in her face when the man standing next to her growled, low and frightening. He looked at him when the man shoved his way into the booth as well.

"This is a little too crowded, don't you think? Why don't you let me go, and we'll have us a nice lunch some other—?" The cop across from him told him now was fine with them. "Look. This is just stupid. Tell me what it is you want, and then I'll tell you no and be on my way. I have things to do today."

"You going to look up your son?" Howie stared at the woman next to him. "You don't have any idea who I am, do you? Not a clue as to where I might have come from."

"No, I don't. Should I? I'm thinking that with a body like yours, I'd remember." The man growled again, and the claw in his hand deepened. "Fuck, that hurts. What the hell are you trying to do to me? Tear my hand off?"

"If I wanted to do that, I would have already. Don't ever talk to the women in this family like that again. Do I make myself clear? Or do you need another reminder on what manners are? You seemed to have forgotten them." He shook his head. "Good. Your son. You know where he is, by any chance?"

"No. I was here to find him. Last I heard, he was here someplace." The woman to his right told him he was dead, along with the rest of his family. "Howard is dead? No. No, that cannot be true."

Even to his ears, it didn't sound like he was the least bit upset about it. The woman to his right told him Howard's wife had been her sister. Then it hit him. His balls were now gone. They'd crawled so far up his ass that he was sure he was going to have to have them surgically removed before he could take a shit. He'd bet right now he couldn't even have a good fart without hurting. Swallowing hard, he asked her when she'd found out.

"Found out? You mean that you killed him? I found out a couple of days ago. Imagine my surprise when I got to speak to Bree, and she told me you had them all locked up in a storage locker with carbon monoxide pouring into the thing." Shaking his head, he cursed when she popped him in the back of it. "Use your words, Howie. Don't be a lazier fuck than I know you already are."

"She has a real problem with people who take shortcuts, Howie. Like when you put your son in the car in the driver's seat. You see,

Howard couldn't drive. He couldn't talk or feed himself. But what was especially telling was that there wasn't any way he could have pulled the trigger on the gun you forgot to leave behind. Howard was unable to even lift the gun. Terrible mistake, that one. He'd had a stroke, which I'm thinking will also be attributed to you, about four months ago. I believe it was right after you took all their food right out of the cabinets and fridge, then sold it off." The man to the right of Bree's sister smiled at him. "I did a little searching on my own, you see. And with the help of a real officer, I was able to get the right information to the police."

"There is no way you'd have that sort of information. They were all dead when I put them in the car." The first woman asked him about Howard. "I killed him in the car. You people are stupid if you think I'm going to believe you spoke to them when—"

It hit him hard that he had just confessed to killing his son. Not only that, but that he'd placed the others in the car with him. Shoving them out of his way, Howie wanted to kill them right then. But getting away so that he could think was the only thing he could actually do. He had no gun with him, nor any way to be able to kill all four of them and get away.

The claw in his hand tore at his flesh when he stood up. Crying out, he ran from the place, holding his hand close to his body as their laughter floated after him.

He'd been staying at a nice hotel in town, waiting for some word about his son. But now, with them knowing who he was and what he'd done, he had to hide. Stopping in the middle of the street, horns blaring around him, Howie realized he was making a mistake in letting them get to him. Yes, he'd confessed, he told himself, but who would believe them? No one.

The badge the other man had laid out—it could have been fake for all the time he'd spent in looking it over. Nor had he been as trapped as they made him feel. Howie had been able to shove himself out of the diner quick enough. No, this was what they wanted him to do. Panic. And panicky people made huge mistakes. But it was the gun that bothered him the most.

Had he left it in the car? Right now, he was beginning to think he'd not. The kids had been silenced. Bree too. She was a good fuck, but all the while he was giving it to her, she was sobbing and wailing like a damned fool. It was almost as bad as fucking his wife he'd had at one time. Laughing, he thought that the old saying of cops being able to get away with murder was truer than any other saying about cops.

Howie had gotten away with it about a dozen times over his lifetime. That brought him around to thinking about his son. Well, he'd been a pussy too. Howard refusing to leave his wife and kids by the side of the road so Howie could live with him had been the final straw. Though now he understood why he didn't speak to him in those last few minutes. He couldn't. Damn, he was glad now that he'd killed him too. Who the hell wanted a cripple around all the time anyway?

A lot of the things that had happened in those few days it had taken him to get rid of the dead weight of his son was making more sense now. Howard hadn't spoken a word to him. And when he'd had to move him from the house to where he'd killed off the others, Howie had had to drag him. He'd thought that Howard was being stubborn, but now he knew the real reason. He couldn't walk.

Howie had hated Bree. Even fucking her, taking her against her will, hadn't endeared her to him at all. And those fucking kids? Christ, they should have thanked him for taking care of them rather than being pissed off by them.

Deciding he needed medical care, he made his way to his car so he could get to the hospital. There was a nice one here in town that he'd been to a couple of times. He just hoped they didn't try and charge him. He didn't have the money to go around paying bills that didn't give him anything in return, like going to the hospital.

There was money in his accounts—also stashed around his home. But at the moment, he couldn't get to his house due to termites. Whoever heard of such a thing of tenting a house to get rid of the vermin. He just killed his pests. But he had money buried in the backyard, as well as in the very car he was in now. Guns were also planted everywhere. Howie didn't want to be caught unawares like he had been this morning.

Bree's sister? What was her name? He knew eventually it would come to him. But now he had to get some help. While he was sure he wouldn't die from blood loss, he couldn't get it to stop bleeding.

After three hours in the waiting room, he was finally taken to a room. Before the nurse left him, he told her he wanted to see someone stitch up his hand now. Not in another three hours. All she did was close the door to his room and leave him there. Howie would have walked out if not for the fact that he was still soaking through paper towels. And the one towel he'd put on it that he'd stolen from the clothesline he'd passed on the way here was so wet with his blood that it weighed about fifty pounds. Not really, but it was soaking wet.

The doctor came in a few minutes later. Howie was beginning to get sick to his belly. It might well have been from hunger, but he wasn't sure. The man took one look at his hand and sat down and said he couldn't sew it up.

"Why the hell not? It's nearly to the bone." The doc asked him if a shifter had done it. "Yeah. Now that I think on it, he had a white paw. And a gun with a fake badge. Biggest fucker I've ever seen, too. What does that have to do with you sewing me up before I bleed to death?"

"It won't heal. Nor will it stop bleeding until you make restitution for whatever it is you did to him. I would say you should go apologize to him, but I'm doubtful that will work." He asked him why not. "It must have been my brother that cut you. He's the only one that carries a badge, which is real, and a gun all the time. Yes, he won't accept your apology anyway. You're Howie Lane, aren't you?"

"Yes." The doctor stood up to leave. "Aren't you going to at least try to seal them up? Damn it, I'm losing a lot of blood here."

"I could glue them closed, but I don't believe that will work anyway." He told him to do it. "Nope. I don't like that you killed two small children and a nice woman and her husband. I just spoke to my brother, Sawyer Bishop, and he said to tell you to fuck off. I'd have told you the same thing, but I do dislike being redundant. He said for you to remember his name because he's going to be coming after you soon. All the police department will be. Also, the Feds. They're good friends of the family, it turns out. Anyway, good luck with trying to find someone that will try to fix that for you. It certainly won't be anyone at this hospital."

Howie just stood there for five minutes, hoping the man was kidding and would return. When the door opened, he smiled, ready to tell the man he liked a good joke like anyone else. But it was billing.

"Mr. Lane? How would you like for us to bill you? If you pay today, you will get a ten percent discount. Would you like to take advantage of that and pay today? We take all major credit cards." He asked her how much they were going to charge him for doing shit for him. "The total comes to just under nine-hundred-and-sixty dollars. You'll save ninety-six dollars if you pay right now."

"You're fucking kidding me. A thousand bucks for just having a crackpot of a doctor coming in here and telling me he's not going to help me?" The woman told him Doctor Bishop was a great doctor and that he should behave himself. "Behave myself? Christ. I'm not paying that. Not today for hundred bucks off, nor at any time you send me a bill. He didn't do shit for me."

"Then I suppose we'll have to turn you over to a collection agency if you refuse to pay." He told her to go right on ahead with it. He was already a member there. "Good day, Mr. Lane."

She left him and left the door open behind her. Howie wasn't going to leave until he got taken care of. However, when security showed up with the police, he left. Christ, if this kept up, someone would find him bled out in his hotel room in a couple of days.

Leaving with a police escort, he was in his car when he decided he'd take care of his wound on his own. The pharmacy had all the things he needed—wraps, antiseptic cream, as well as tape. While standing in line waiting for his turn, he saw glue, the kind that could hold a man's weight up on a ceiling. Buying several tubes of it, he paid for it all and made his way back to the hotel.

Cleaning the wound was difficult, as all it did was bleed more under the water. Leaning over the tub, he dried the cuts and then squeezed an entire tube of the smelly stuff into the first long cut.

Falling back on his ass, screaming his fool head off, he wished now he'd thought to pick up a bag of ice. No one had warned him that the fucking glue hurt worse than the cuts did. Hitting his head on the commode, he was out.

~*~

Dwayne knew that both Brit and Jamie had slept badly. He could hear the little boy crying out and his mom racing down to his room. He had wanted to go, wanted to help however he could. But when he'd started to follow her, Brit told him she had it and for him to go back to bed. Going into his bedroom, he knew he wasn't going to sleep now and decided to get some work done.

The sun was coming up when he reached for his brother Quincey. Dwayne invited him to have breakfast with him at his house. Quincey said he'd like that, and they agreed to meet in twenty minutes. Just about enough time, Dwayne thought, for him to form his questions for him.

"Good morning. How long have you been up?" Brit always brought a smile to his face when she just came near him. Feeling sappy, he told her he'd been up for a while. He didn't want her thinking she'd awakened him for good when Jamie had cried out. "Jamie is getting up too. He's not sleeping well, as you know. I'm hoping I can get him in to see Quincey this morning to get something for him to rest."

"He's coming here for breakfast with us." She smiled at him again and went to the kitchen. Following her, he saw Jamie coming down the stairs. He looked terrible. "My brother is coming over to see you this morning, buddy. Hopefully, we can work something out that will have you feeling better."

"I was going to talk to you about that. I was wondering if you could fix me up." Dwayne asked him what he meant. "How Raven and Sawyer fixed Molly. I'm really dying here, Dwayne. My head hurts when I try to sleep because I'm a back sleeper. My teeth hurt too. And I can't see much of anything because everything is so blurry.

Quincey said that could be an option, but at the time, we didn't have Mom there to tell him it would be all right."

"That's something you'll need to talk about with your mom, buddy. That's not something that can just be done without consequences. If she agrees, I'll help you. Otherwise, you're going to have to suffer like all other humans I know."

Both of them laughed, but he could tell Jamie was in pain. Even touching his forehead to get his hair out of his eyes had him moaning.

As soon as his brother arrived, Dwayne hugged him. Asking him about his night, Quincey told them how Howie had come in to get his hand stitched up. He was laughing almost too hard for them to understand him.

"Then he arrived by ambulance last night. He'd been in his hotel on the floor after falling and bumping his head on the toilet just after he'd been at the hospital, I guess. A little over a week ago. But that wasn't what caused the entire staff at the hospital to laugh. He'd put an entire tube of that monkey glue—I don't remember the name—right into his cut. Christ, that must have hurt." Jamie told him what it was called. "That's it. Right. The only way to get that stuff out of his wound was to cut it out. Like cutting the flesh that was covered with it off and then covering him up like he was a burn victim. And it's still bleeding from what Sawyer had done to him. I tell you right now, that man is all kinds of stupid."

"Stupid and dangerous." Brit sat down with them with a cup of hot tea. "I have a question before we get too deep into the intelligence of Howie Lane. I would like to know if it is possible for someone—I'm assuming it would have to be Dwayne—to give him some of their blood. He's not healing quickly enough for me to feel good about leaving him to go to New York."

"You're going home without me?" Jamie looked at her, then at him. "What did you do to her that she's leaving? Did you hurt her after promising me you'd not? Figures. You—"

"That's enough." Dwayne looked at Brit. "Can you tell him why you're going back to your home? I'd like to not be the bad guy for you two." Brit looked as shocked as he felt. Looking at Jamie, he told him what was going on. "She's going home to pack up yours and her place so she can work from here. We've figured out a way for her to start transferring her merchandise to here slowly and still have the warehouse there. Christ. Do either of you ever check out what is really going on before you start pointing your finger at the innocent person in the room?"

Getting up, he thanked his brother for coming over this morning, then told him he was sorry he'd had to witness that. Leaving by the front door, he was in his car and down the road before Quincey contacted him.

While I don't blame you for leaving – that was harsh – could you please return and give Jamie some of your blood? Or I could do it. His mom is upstairs sobbing. I can hear her from the kitchen, where I still am. Jamie is crying too, but he's more pissed off at himself than anything. Do they do this to you all the time? He told him just the one time before. *I don't know if I could stand that, being a bad guy all the time. By the way, Brit had some pretty harsh words for her son after you left. She was royally pissed at him.*

Good. I'm turning around now. I don't like this either. I know they both have a great many trust issues, but I've done nothing wrong at all. Quincey said he knew he hadn't. *I'm nearly back. Tell Jamie for me that I'm going to do this, but I don't want to talk to him. I'm still hurting.*

Dwayne was nearly to the kitchen when Brit came down the stairs. She had been crying. When she wrapped her arms around him and told him how sorry she was for what her son had said, he held her to him. When he kissed her on top of her head, she looked up at him.

"Jamie lashing out at you is my fault." He said it wasn't. "It is. I had no one to unburden myself to, and he was there. I told him things… well, it's small wonder he doesn't trust people. He's been told by his mom that she'll never trust someone again."

"What about me? Where do I fall in this line of terrible people who did terrible things to you? I need to know if this is going to be a battle I have to fight all the time. If it is, I can't do this. It's too much." She told him he was right. It was too much for her too. "I'm not going to make you trust me, Brit, but a little consideration would be nice. I've never hurt you or Jamie. And I don't think I've given either of you cause to not trust me. Have I?"

"No. And I'm going to start believing my heart over my head from now on. You're a wonderful person. I don't know that I would have returned, but you did, and I can't tell you how much that means to me." Jamie said it did to him as well. "You owe Dwayne an apology, young man."

"I do. Not just for today, but for a lot of

things I've been thinking too." Dwayne looked at his brother, who just shook his head. No, he was telling him, he'd not had anything to do with what Jamie was saying. Coming toward him, Jamie spoke again. "You've been the best person to me, and I've been a little shit." Jamie glanced at his mother. "I have been."

"You're not going to get any kind of disagreement from me. I have been as well." Jamie looked up at him, and, letting go of Brit, Dwayne got down to his level before speaking to him.

"I'm so sorry. Sorrier than I've been about anything, even things that hurt my mom—this is me being sorrier than ever." Jamie wrapped his arms around his neck and hugged him tightly. "I'm not doing this as a suck up. Quincey told me to tell you that right off. But I'm asking you if you'd allow me to call you Dad. I know you're going to have to think about it. Who would want such a rotten kid to be—?"

"Nothing would make me happier than to have you call me Dad." Hugging the two of them, he felt his own eyes fill with tears as they hugged. "As your father, I should punish you, but I think you've had enough trauma for one lifetime. If it's all right with your mom, I'll help you out with the wounds now too. I was going to anyway, but now, being your dad, I feel proud to do it."

Quincey walked him through how to lick the wounds closed. Dwayne was slightly afraid of this method and was thrilled when Brit told him to give him some of his blood. Licking such a huge wound closed so near the brain wasn't anything he'd ever done before. Even if Jamie were his biological son, he thought he'd still have trouble with it.

Taking a knife from Quincey to open a wound, he cut slightly into his finger and let several drops fall onto Jamie's tongue. Quincey told him to stop when he realized he might well have given him too much. Jamie sat on the couch with his eyes closed and a smile on his face as they watched him.

"I can touch my head to the back of the couch now. It feels amazing." Brit laughed and asked him if he was going to take a nap. "I think I might. But I just want to feel this for a little while to remember how it felt."

"I'd like to check your wound before you go to la-la land. I think that's what Dad calls his nap time." Quincey had pulled the staples out before Dwayne gave Jamie blood. Smiling, he looked at him. "It's already healed. Even the hair that needed to be shaved off is growing back. I would like to check on you tomorrow, so come by my office. But I think you're going to be just fine, Jamie. However, I want you to still take it easy. Our blood is very strong, and I haven't any idea how it might affect you." Quincey said he'd see them later and headed home.

"Thanks, Dad. I feel wonderful." Dwayne felt him being called Dad all the way to his heart and spilling over. It was so full of love for the kid. "Mom, is it still all right that I stay here while you're gone to New York? What did the landlord say?"

"I fired him. Right after I bought the building." Both Jamie and Brit stared at Dwayne with open mouths. "What? He was enforcing rules that were not very nice. Also, he was charging more rent from you and the other tenants, double what the owner had set in place for him to collect. Also, the water rule? The owner thought it was just as ludicrous as we all did. So, your mom is going back to collect her things from the house and have them brought here, then she's going to spend a day making arrangements with her job. Mr. Little, I think you met him, he's going with her to help set up cameras in the warehouse, as well as a better computer system here and there so she can work from anyplace."

"What do you mean, anyplace?" Brit answered Jamie as in anyplace. "So, if we were to take that cruise we've been talking about forever, you could work from there too? I mean, not miss a client or anything?"

"That's what it means." Jamie left them then to go up to the room he'd been using before Brit stopped him. "I'm going to need to know what sort of things you want from your old bedroom. All right? Make a list."

"When you get there, you can video chat with me, and that way, I can tell you when I see the stuff. Wow, does that mean I'm going to someday have more brothers and sisters? This is so cool. I can't wait to tell GGMa Holly. She'll bust a gut." He was still laughing as he went out of sight.

"Well? Does this mean he can have more brothers and sisters?" Dwayne told her that was up to her. "I'd love to have an entire houseful of them. Just not all at one time."

"You do know we're going to have to have sex in order for that to happen." Brit told him she knew how it worked. "I'm just saying. When would you like to start on his family of his?"

"When I get back. I need to get this settled up and have my own things around me. I'm sorry. I shouldn't have teased you like that." He told her it was fine, and she smiled at him. "I hope so. As soon as I get back, I'm going to rock you until the sun comes up and more if I can manage it."

"I'll help you." Kissing her again, feeling her pent-up need, Dwayne walked to the front door. "I'll be home for supper. Raven said the plane is all ready to go anytime you want to leave."

"The sooner I go, the quicker I can get back." This time she kissed him. "Will you be all right here with Jamie? He's going to be raring to go now that he's feeling better."

"We'll be fine. If he gets to be too much for me, I'll take him to my parents. They'll love having him over. Especially when he calls them his grandparents."

This time he did leave the house. Already late for the office, he sat at his desk and was ready to go. It wasn't until he looked at his computer and saw the date that he realized why he'd not seen anyone in the building but security. It was Saturday. Shaking his head at his confusion, he decided to do a little shopping. Jamie needed a phone. Also, a winter coat that he could wear until his mom got back. Calling the house, he told Brit what he'd done and what he was planning.

"Good. You guys can take me to the airport. I've just decided I'll leave now and be back sooner."

He drove home. Dwayne also realized she'd need something to get around in. Pulling off the side of the road, he pulled out his notebook and wrote things down. It was going to be a blast hanging out with Jamie, he thought.

Chapter 4

Brit was glad for the extra hands in getting things packed up. Raven and the other women had come along with her when they found out where she was going. Then, when she'd begged off from their shopping spree, they decided to help her so she could go with them. They were going to use her apartment as a stashing place for things they didn't want to carry.

"All done. The homeless shelter will be here first thing on Monday to take the furniture and the boxes of clothing. That was nice of you to think of them." She nodded, distracted from what Penny was saying to her. "Are you upset about the fact you're giving this all away? We can cancel them coming if you want."

"No, it's not that. I think this is the best

way to deal with this stuff. I'm missing some things. Not a lot, just some things I could have sworn were here." Andi entered the room and sat down on the couch that was going too. "I don't suppose you saw a photo album, did you? It's pictures of my parents when they were alive."

"Your landlord took it. Along with about ten pairs of your panties and some other personal items. Did you know he was a crossdresser?" Brit asked her if she was serious. "I am. I can even tell you what color of your panties he has on right now if you want."

"No thanks. What I meant was, why would he take things from me? I think he's married, right?" She did that thing with her hand that meant she was sort of right. "I usually bust people's chops for doing that sort of thing, but you scare the living daylights out of me. What do you mean? Is he married or not?"

"He is, but they're not really a couple. She has affairs, and he watches them. In a dress that belongs to Mrs. Carter down the hall." Brit sat down. "Are you really afraid of me? I wish you wouldn't be. I'd never hurt you."

"Yes, I'm afraid of you. Of all of you, to be honest. I'm the only human in the bunch, and even though I was told I was immortal, I still think you could put me in a world of hurt. Back to Mr. Black. Not that I want my things back, thank you very much, but how long has he been doing this?" She told her. "Christ, that's a very long time. Fifty years? So, since I know he's fifty-six, he's been a crossdresser for all this time, and I had no idea."

"I think you met him once when he was dressed up. You said you had the same dress she had on." Brit remembered it, how she thought the woman was very manly but hadn't said anything. "Yes, if you're thinking that—it was your dress. You had given it to one of the charities around here the week before."

"This is all too much." She looked around. "The only thing I want back is the photo album. Can you, I don't know, twitch your nose and get it for me?"

"Yes." When she put her fingers to her nose and "twitched" it, the album appeared on Brit's lap. "I don't normally twitch my nose, but you were beginning to freak out. Have you ever noticed how much we say that? Anyway, you have it, and I'm starving. How about, since we're done here, we go and get us something good to eat that is totally terrible for us?"

She was ready to eat as well. Brit hadn't

really packed all that much to take back to Ohio with her—their clothing, the few pictures hanging on the wall that she had picked up here and there. The computer Jamie had in his room wasn't worth saving. Mr. Little—Matthew, he'd told her to call him—showed her how old it was. So she had him wipe it clean, and they were donating it as well.

There were no pets, no plants, and nothing endearing to her about the place she and her son had lived in for the last ten years. Looking around one last time, as they were going to spend the next two days in a hotel, she didn't have one bit of nostalgia for the place. It had been a place for them to stay warm. The place had never been warm to them, Jamie told her when she talked to him earlier.

Penny stood next to her like she was thinking of something, then snapped her fingers and smiled at her before speaking. "Dwayne should have taken your blood before we left, and you two could have spoken. Wait, we can fix that. Andi?"

When she was ready to ask what was going on, Brit found herself in the living room of Dwayne's brother's home, and a loud football game was on the big screen. She stumbled into his arms when she "landed," she thought it might be called.

"I should have thought of this before." He took her hand to his mouth and kissed it before biting deeply into her skin. It really didn't hurt, but she could feel something different. Offering up his hand to her, she looked at his blood as it pooled in his palm. Licking it, feeling the dizzying effects of it, she was back in New York, almost where she'd disappeared.

Now that I can speak to you without having to go through the others, I want you to have a good time. Jamie and I have gone shopping here. He now has a nice heavy winter coat that he's out in the snow playing with Molly in. Also, boots. So if you were planning on picking those up, we have them.

I'll mark them off my list. He will need a desk and a place to do his homework. Which reminds me. I don't know anything about the schools there. Where does Molly go? He told her. *Will the pack school take Jamie too?*

Yes. I hope you don't mind, but I've already talked about it with the pack leader, and they're all for it. Also, I'm not sure you're aware of this or not, but Holly got him a laptop that he's been using in the room he's been in. Which, I'm to tell you, is the one he wants to keep. Something about the view. The only thing I could see that he'd be looking at is in Gunner's backyard. Unless it's the animals there. She told him it was and marked the computer off her list. *What else can I do for you, so you have some fun? Do you have ornaments? I have a few dozen, but not enough to cover the tree we're going to have. It's going to be monstrous. As in at least fifteen feet tall.*

My goodness. No, I don't have any. Jamie and I had this old ceramic one that we used, but it bit the dust while we were packing up. Not that I was going to use it anymore. I want a large Christmas too. How do you do Thanksgiving? I'm betting it's huge. This year especially. He told her it would be. *Good. I don't remember the last time Jamie and I had one. We usually went out to eat, but that got to be boring too after a few years. I can't think of anything else. I'm going to see if they have some ornaments I can pick up. Anything special?*

No. Mom gave me some of the things I did for her when I was in school. Not many, mind you, as we were homeschooled until we were old enough to see the world, she told us. I was able to skip grades four through being a few months shy of graduation. All of us were like that. She told him she was proud of him. *Thanks. All right, my dear lovely future wife, you have a good time. We're on the four-yard line here and behind by two points. I have to see this ending.*

Looking around as to where they were, she decided that nothing could be better than hanging out with a bunch of women, with all the Christmas displays up already. She decided she was going to do a little shopping for things for the family as well. What do you get, she wondered, for a family that seemed to have it all? Brit knew she could figure it out. And she'd have fun doing it too.

"I don't want to embarrass you or anything, but I wanted to talk to you about money." Holly, who had flown in later with Sippy and met them at the store, spoke to her when they were alone. "Dwayne is going to take over my business when I'm ready to let go. The way he's working, it'll be a lot sooner than I thought when I started. I'm thrilled, don't get me wrong. I have so many plans with— Yes, get to the point. I pay him very well."

"Thank you. I make good money too." Holly nodded. "But that's not what you're trying so hard to tell me, is it? I'm better if you just give it to me straight. You think I'm spending too much of his money. I assure you, I'm not. I'm only using my credit cards and—"

"That's it. You see, I noticed you're putting things on your credit card. Are you one of those people that says he pays some bills from his account, and you pay the rest from yours?" She said she'd never thought of it before. "I've always been a component of the money goes into a single pot, and we all use it. Dwayne's last commission check alone was nearly four million dollars. The one before that was considerably more."

"Considerably more than four million." Holly nodded and smiled at her. "I see. Sort of. How much is Dwayne worth? Or is this a question I should be putting to him?"

"Him, I would say. I think the two of you should talk, but the reason I bring it up is that I believe you're not having fun. I do love that you're checking prices and going to the clearance rack. My goodness, I do that too. All of us do. Especially Raven." She huffed. "I'm nervous, and I'm rarely that way, so I'm getting sidetracked. What I'm saying is, you should have fun and purchase all the things you want. Not regardless of the price—no, I don't mean that. But you should buy your son that game system you were looking at. Also, I know for a fact that Gunner would love that pipe holder. I've only just noticed that he's collecting them. I do love that boy—all of them, very much. Talk to Dwayne, child. I'm sure the two of you are long overdue for a nice sit-down."

With a pat on her back, Holly left her there. Looking around the store at the women that she'd come with, she did notice that their piles were larger than hers. Also, they were having a great time. She was pinching pennies so tightly they were screaming.

I need to talk to you. Brit smiled and asked him if Holly had spoken to him. *Yes. Well, spoken to is using the term loosely. She told me I need to get my butt in gear and talk to you. So, here I am talking to you. I have…we have money. Too much of it, I think sometimes. But there is a great deal of it. Not counting my commission checks, I make a nice salary. Okay, I make an obscene amount of money. I invest well, and…I'm screwing this all up. I'm sorry. It never occurred to me that this was something we should talk about before you left. I've never had a mate before.*

Neither have I. Jamie and I used to have nothing until I hit on this idea that I could collect the uncollectable and make it work for us. Thus the name of my warehouse. Uncollectable Merchandise. Dwayne told her he'd not even known that. *As Holly pointed out, we've not spoken much. Mostly it's me yelling at you about something you didn't do.*

We're past that, right? She said she was but

could still feel bad about it. *No. Please don't. If we're past it, then we are. Besides, I'm a dad now, so I feel like I'm unstoppable. But for money. I'm getting close to what Raven has, which I think is all the money. I listen when she or Sawyer talk about what they're doing. I also watch the market and take my cues from Holly. She's taught me a great deal about the business world.*

My learning curve has been fail and attempt again for the most part. They both laughed. *Holly asked me if I was the type that put it all in a pot, and we both use it. When Herman was around, if it went into any kind of pot, he'd take it. So I'll leave it up to you about how we do our money. Which I have a bit of too. I have invested well, but I don't have nearly the amount that it sounds like you do.*

We have billions of dollars. More than a normal person could spend in their lifetime. I'd like to say that was all we need to worry about, but I'm sure you're like me in thinking we need to continue to work just in case. I don't know what problem there would be, but I don't want to be wishing I'd not retired so soon. Or that we wished we had more money. Immortality makes a person think how long that really is. She knew that too. It was something she worried about. *Raven told me you didn't save much in the way of things at your old place. If you think I might be upset about bringing things back to the house, I won't. Bring home whatever you want.*

It's not that. After really looking hard at the things we had, I realized how worn, and in terrible shape it all was. Even our towels were just about in threads. I don't think I've purchased anything new for us in longer than I care to admit. Dwayne told her he was sorry about that. *Yes, me too. But we don't have a great deal to sort through when I get back. And Mr. Little is doing a great job on the business computer. He's even programmed my phone with a way to get orders or messages, and he's going to set my computers up there. This will make my job so much easier. Not to mention, I'm having someone come in and look to see if they can fix some of the things for me, so they work.*

You said they'll be happier with the things that will work for them. I think this is an awesome business plan you have for yourself. He laughed. *All right. I have to get off here. I love you, Brit. I'll see you in a couple of days.*

After the brief conversation with Dwayne, she did have fun. For the next couple of days, she was going to take care of the warehouse things, shop, and enjoy herself. It was really nice to be able to not worry about working or what might be going on there. After a brief lesson, showing

Dwayne how to check the inventory for what might be needed and the price list for the daily work, he had been keeping an eye on things for her. And she was planning on enjoying herself too.

~*~

"His arm had to be removed from the elbow down. There might be more damage done that we'll have to deal with. But for now, that's where we are. I never would have thought this would happen. I thought for sure we had cleaned all the glue off his hand." Dwayne asked his brother what he meant, more damage. "When he put that glue into an open wound, especially as much as he did, it was bad enough. Then no one found him in his room. Then gangrene set in, and his fingers had already lost blood flow for several days. Had he not put out the do not disturb sign when he went into his room, he might well have been found sooner. As it was, he had spent nine days lying there, in and out of consciousness, drinking water from the tub when he could get to it, thankfully, or he would never have survived, with the poison from the glue making its way through his bloodstream."

"Christ. What the hell did he think was going to happen when he did something that dumb? Especially without a medical staff right there with him." Quincey said he had told him all he needed to do was to talk to and apologize to Sawyer, and he could heal it. "So, since he knew that sometimes glue is used to seal larger wounds, he decided he knew better and used something like he did on his own. What a fucking moron."

"He could lose his arm entirely with this. I'm also concerned about his heart. The man was a mess even before the thing with the glue." Dwayne asked if he'd spoken to the police about it. "I have. They've taken precautions that he doesn't get up and out on his own. They have fudged the evidence they found with the storage container, as well as the information from Howard's doctor, and made sure they're digging deeper on things. Not fudged in that they're lying about it, but how they found the container. They're saying they were led there by an unnamed source. I think that would be the best way to deal with this, don't you?"

"I do. Howard, I was told, moved on, but his wife is sticking around. She and Brit have spoken a couple of times about funeral arrangements. If that isn't the oddest thing I've ever heard of. Bree is helping her sister finalize her family's resting place. Also, she helped with the marker for them. It's nice, I guess. Sort of like preplanning after the fact." He shivered. "To change the subject, how much do you know about movie props?"

"Props? Do you mean like Brit does for a living? To be honest with you, Dwayne, I've never thought of it in any serious kind of way. Why?" He pulled up the inventory Brit had to make her business work, then showed him the pictures of each item from different angles so that people, media people, could see what they wanted. "She even has it in date groupings. Christ, does she really have a 747? How the hell would someone go about getting one of those?"

"I asked her. She said there is a website that sells off surplus army things. Every time they have a sale, Brit looks there to see what she can find. She has two full planes, as well as just the body of one. They're stored on a different lot that she bought some years ago. Believe it or not, it's close to here. Right now, we're having a building put up that she is designing herself that will house the things she purchases. Even Mom and Andi's things are on this site that Mom is willing to rent out when they need things too."

"This is very lucrative for all of them then?"

Dwayne showed them the prices for just an old couch for three months. "Wouldn't it be cheaper to just have the set crew make one? I mean, five grand for three months—that seems like a great deal of money."

"I asked that too. But what I didn't think of, nor did you, I think, was what are they supposed to do with it once the movie is over? That's another thing she buys—old sets of sitcoms that have stopped. Also, food containers, like boxes of cereal, labels that had come off cans. I'm amazed at this crap." Quincey just shook his head at it all. "While I've been watching her business for her, she's had two calls for a bedroom suite from the seventies, as well as a kitchen from the eighties. While I have no idea what that would entail, the people that called didn't even hesitate long enough to ask me prices. Just delivery dates, as well as when they had to be returned. Also, most of the rented things will be brought back to her new warehouse here instead of in New York."

"She's amazing. I hope you tell her that all the time." Dwayne said he was going to when she got back. "Good. I have to get back to the hospital. I only came home long enough to get myself a shower and clean clothes. I'll let you know—"

When Quincey's cell phone went off, he said it was the hospital. Leaving him there to work on his paperwork, Quincey returned long enough to let him know that Howie was headed to surgery again. They found another blood clot in his legs. After he was gone, Dwayne decided not to tell Brit while she was away unless it was about his passing. He didn't want to ruin her fun.

Throughout the rest of the afternoon, one or more of his family would show up and talk to him, then leave again. When his dad showed up close to two o'clock, he yelled at him for working all the time when he had family that wanted to hang out with him. He said he was bored with Brit gone and that Jamie was with Grandma at his home.

"No reason for you to be working, regardless of where everyone is. Besides, I have some things I want to run by you while they're gone. I have a new rose garden going in at the new house. Also, a nice garden that your mom has been after me about. I was wondering if you'd come over and show me what goes where. I have a list of stuff she wants around the house, but I can't make heads or tails of how to put it together so it'll look good."

"I'd look to see how tall things are." Dad

looked at him oddly. "Well, I'm sure she doesn't want the little bitty things planted in the back where they're going to be overshadowed by the taller flowers. Are these flowers annuals or perennials?"

"Here." Dad handed him the list. "How do you know how tall those things are going to be anyway? Not to mention, how would you make them look good? There seems to be a lot of different colors there." Dwayne pulled up snapdragons and saw that they could get to be about thirty inches tall. "What does that mean about them being tender?"

"They're perennials, but they usually can't survive a winter and don't come back. I'm thinking she'll want them planted someplace that she can get to easily so she can replace them if they don't make it. Like out around the barn you guys are having put in." Dad nodded and watched Dwayne as he pulled up flower after flower, putting not only how tall they were when they were in full bloom, but whether they were yearly or forever plants, as Dad called them, and the color of them. "This will be a chart that Mom and you can use all the time. Like when you buy Mom flowers, you can use this list when you want to perhaps change it out for a plant that she can have around to remind her that you love her so very much."

"I do." Dad blew his nose and looked at him with watery eyes. "I do love that woman to distraction. I owe you, son, for this. Every time I have me a gander at it, I'll remember us sitting here working on it together."

Hugging his dad, Dwayne asked him if he wanted to order anything more than what Mom already had. Mom hadn't gotten anything on her list as yet, but the things she did want were only a touch away to be ordered on the Internet. Dad even had an account now where he could simply order Mom things and make it so all the information she wanted on whatever Dad had ordered today or in the future was right there for her to use as well.

Dad ended up ordering everything on the list Mom had given him. In addition to that, he ordered a few things Dwayne told him went well with the plants he'd ordered. After making sure the company had his address for where to send them when the time to plant came along, Dad asked him to lunch.

"That would be great. Having dinner with my favorite dad." Dad glared at him, then laughed. "How about the rest of them? Or would you rather it be just the two of us?"

"I won't ever turn down a meal with my kids. No matter how old you all get." Dad stood up. "I tell you what, why don't you get that son of yours, and we'll have us a manly time."

Dad left him sitting there with, Dwayne was sure, his mouth hanging open. His son. Jamie was already calling him Dad and his parents his grandparents, but to have someone point out that he had a son nearly had him sobbing. Christ, he thought, he was getting sappy. Reaching out to his son, he asked Jamie if he wanted to have lunch with them. It was several seconds before he answered him, and when he did, Dwayne had to sit down.

Don't freak out. All right? Dwayne told him he already was. *Just breathe for me, Dad. In and out. I'm hurt, but not like my head was. But I hurt me, and I'm worried that you and Mom will freak out when you see it when you see us. Also –*

More than likely, we will. Where are you, and has my mom seen it yet? Dwayne told him he was in the barn, and no, Grandma hadn't seen it yet. *Can you walk? Wait, what did you mean, us? Is there someone there with you, Jamie?*

Yes. The pause had him yelling for his dad. *Dad, Uncle Wesley is here too. He's hurt. Not dead, but hurt. I was working up to it so you could come to help us and not hurt yourself getting here. Can you come here? I'm afraid for Grandma to see us. She'll be too upset. Bring Grandda too. I think we'll need him.*

We're on our way. I'm going to send Quincey to you as well. Just keep an eye out for one of the tigers in the event that they will get them to you sooner. He said he wasn't afraid of them. *All right. Also, when we get there, we'll figure out what happened that had you both hurt. Unless you know now.*

He and Dad were getting into Dad's car as he spoke to Jamie. Not only did Jamie know what had happened, but he thought perhaps it was his fault that Wesley was hurt. He told him again that he could see him breathing and that he wasn't dead.

I was helping him reclean the plow. I think that's what it's called. I'm too upset to remember right now. Mr. Millner called and asked if Uncle Wesley could help him turn some dirt for next season. It sure is dark dirt. Dwayne told him to continue. *Right. Uncle Wesley was pulling the piece to where we'd gotten it when I fell into the board. I was pushing because we thought it would be easier than me – it's the thing that turns the dirt. When I fell back, I grabbed for Uncle Wesley and pulled him into the plow. There is a lot of blood under him. Please don't freak out. Okay?*

That'll make me freak out, and I don't think that will be a good thing, do you?

No. Not for anyone. Quincey told him he was nearly there. Sawyer was with Chandler, and they were pulling into the drive now. *All right, son. The troops are there. You have to remain calm as well. All right?*

Yes. Dad, don't be angry with me, all right? I love you. He told him he loved him to the depth of his heart. *I surely hope so. I'm starting to hurt a lot now.*

I'm nearly there too, son. You just hang on, Jamie. I want you safe. He said he was now that his uncles were there. *Grandda and I are pulling into the driveway now too. Grandma will be coming out there as soon as she sees us all there. Just tell her how much you love her, and you'll be fine. More than fine.*

Dwayne hoped both of them were fine. He knew in his head they were both immortal, but his heart was telling him that his son was hurt and he needed him. As soon as he entered the barn, he held onto Jamie for a few minutes before he was able to let him go. Then he asked about Wesley.

Chapter 5

Brit kept an eye on Penny while they were in the emergency room. They wouldn't allow her to go back to his cubical until they had him stable, whatever the fuck that meant. When she looked at her again, Brit knew she was going to lose her shit and didn't want that to happen to anyone.

Taking her by the arm, she went through the doors to the rooms, yelling for Wesley just as security tried to keep her from going deeper into the room. She looked him right in the eye and spoke without raising her voice.

"How much insurance do you have for your other half to collect when I'm finished with you?" He didn't look as if he was understanding her, so she smiled. "Will your family that you leave behind have enough to bury you? Or will they need to tap the government for some help? Whatever they need, I want you to know I'll gladly go to prison for putting your family in that position if you try and detain me."

He stared at her for several seconds as his hand on her arm slowly began to release. When it finally occurred to him that she wasn't kidding him, he didn't just release her but asked her where she was headed. That he'd make sure she got there if she didn't hurt him.

"Wesley Bishop. This is his wife, and he's my brother-in-law." Nodding once, he guided them to the room that Wesley was in. Penny went ahead of him as she turned to the man. "Thank you for your help. I want you to know I would have regretted hurting you, but I would have if it came down to that."

"I could see that." He put out his hand, and she took it into hers. She knew immediately that he wasn't human. "Vampire. Samuel. Only name I go by since I can remember. I'm very old and very powerful. I would have hurt you more should you have tried to harm me, but it didn't come down to that, so I'm happy we can part ways as friends. You need anything, Brit, you just call my name, and I'll be there. I have known the Bishops for a good deal longer than either you or your father-in-law."

"I'm Dwayne's mate. He's with my son." Samuel nodded but didn't release her hand as yet. "There is more, isn't there? What is it so I can deal with it, please?"

"You and Dwayne need to bond. Soon. As well as a great deal of magic, I can see things in the future that others cannot. You will need it soon too." She asked him who was after her. "No one. Just in the wrong place at the wrong time, much like your son was today. They'll both live, but that isn't anything to do with me. In that, bonding will make you both safer. You, because of the powerful magic, and Dwayne's cat will be much calmer than now, and he'll not be so jealous. Wesley is a good man as well."

"They all are." He nodded and released her hand. "You've done something to me. I can feel it as it moves along my skin. Is it something I need to be worried about? Or that I should kill you for?"

He threw back his head and laughed. Smiling at him, she asked him if he laughed all that often. It didn't seem to her like he was very good at it. Shaking her hand again, he said he wasn't.

"I've not laughed like that for a very long time. I was laughing at the fact that I just told you I could harm you, and you still think to threaten me." He laughed again. "I should like to see you in a fight one day. However, not today. You have enough going on without me messing up your pretty face. Go to your son and husband. However, be mindful of the information I have given you, and bond soon."

"We will."

He left her there. Not like he moved down the hall and out of her sight, but simply disappeared. However, she did hear his laughter. It echoed around her like a soft blanket. His laughter, like the feeling of something warming her from his magic, was something more that he'd given her. Something powerful too.

As she entered the room where her loves were, Jamie started telling her how sorry he was.

"You didn't do anything." She sat down on the side of his bed and held onto both his and Dwayne's hands. "You're getting care, and you're going to be fine. That's all a mother can ask for in this sort of situation."

She put her hand on his head to pull him closer to kiss him on the cheek. The moment her fingers laced into his hair, she felt a surge of something move from her to both of them. It took her several moments to understand that they were yelling at her to wake up before she realized she'd been out. Looking at the two of them, Dwayne asked her if she was all right.

"I met a vampire named Samuel. He said we needed to bond, and soon." Sitting up, only just realizing she had fallen back, Brit brushed against Jamie's leg and asked if she'd hurt him.

"No. Not at all." He wiggled his foot, then looked at her. "It doesn't hurt at all. Not even a twinge."

"Let me have a look at it. Just so you know, when I helped to pick up my brother, I pulled something in my back. Not badly, but enough to know I picked up something I wasn't used to anymore. It doesn't hurt either." After he cut away the bandage with his knife, he looked at the wound, then at her. "You healed him completely. I mean, there aren't any stitches where they were put in either. It's all gone. You did that, Brit."

"He didn't tell me what he'd given me. Just laughed." Dwayne told her Samuel had had a very difficult life. He'd lost not only his mate but his kiss as well, to a mob some years ago. "He didn't tell me anything. Do you think I can heal your brother? They said he'd lost a great deal of blood and that he won't be able to shift for a while. I'm going to go and see if I can help him."

"Jamie, will you be all right for a few minutes?" Jamie didn't even look up from his leg and the thread, the ones that had stitched him up until he said his name again. "Are you all right, son?"

"I'm healed. My mom did it." Dwayne told him they'd be back in a couple of minutes, then asked if he'd be all right until then. "Yes. I'm better than fine right now. I don't hurt at all."

They left him there, still talking about how he didn't hurt. It had taken all she could muster up to leave her little boy right then. However, she needed to help anywhere she could. Westley was hurt. If she could help, she was going to do it.

Wesley looked terrible, as pale as the sheets covering him. When she said his name, he looked up at her and smiled. Then he asked if Jamie was all right.

"Yes. Better now. I've met a vampire named Samuel." After telling them what had happened and how she'd healed Jamie, it was Penny who asked her to try and do the same for Wesley. "I can and I will if this magic works for him. However, I'd very much like for Dwayne to try. It only just occurred to me that as we share all the magic, he might well have the same thing I have. The ability to heal."

"Try it, son." Saul held her hand while Dwayne put his hand on his brother's chest. It was a couple of seconds before Westley rose up, sitting upright on the bed. The color was back in his cheeks, and he looked better. "My goodness gracious. Just have a look at him."

He did look better. As Dwayne started to fall backwards, unconscious, it was Westley that grabbed him. Pulling him into the bed with him, Westley pulled the gown open by ripping it. Not only was he healed, but there was a small mark on his chest that looked like a small heart. It seemed to call to her as she stood there with Saul, and she put her finger onto it. The heart meant that he was forever loved. Closing her eyes from the overwhelming feelings she got from it, she spoke to the others in the room.

"Westley fell onto the plow trying to get to Jamie. He was going to shift and change him if it came to that. I would have been all right with that, so you all know if it were to save his life." Westley asked her what else she could see. "When you fell on the plow, you were stabbed in the heart. It wouldn't have killed you, but you wouldn't have been the same man you are. Your cat, he would have died from the wound you received if you had been able to fully shift."

"I can feel him. I mean, I can always feel him, but he's getting stronger as I am. You're right, I think. We both would have been injured, and my cat, the part of me that helps me be what I am, would have died from the plow hitting him in his heart." Pulling her hand away from his chest, he pulled her to him and hugged her tightly. "You're special. Even without the ability to shift, I think you're the best of all of us right now. You saved me from certain pain for the rest of my life. I love you, Brit. I cannot ever repay you for what you've given me and my family."

When Dwayne woke up, he smiled at her. They were hugging when Jamie came into the room. Instead of coming to her, he made his way to Wesley and told him how much he loved him. The two of them were still hugging when the doctor came into the room with the paperwork for Jamie to go home.

She was blessed, she thought. Never would she be able to look at these people the same way that she had before. They were and forever would be her family. A family, not just because she was going to marry one of them, but they were family of her heart. Which meant so much more to her.

~*~

Dwayne had plans for this evening. As much as he wanted to go home and get a start on wooing and making love to Brit, he needed to speak to Howie. The little bit of his future that he could see had him dealing with the man that had brought him Brit. It was, he realized, the only reason he was still alive after killing his son and his family. When he woke up, Dwayne let out a long breath he'd been holding unknowingly.

"You're one of them Bishop men. Did you have anything to do with them taking my arm off?" Dwayne told him that was all on him. "Sure it is. That brother of yours, he cut me up bad, and I had to do something, or I'd bleed to death. What are you doing here? You gonna take more from me?"

"No. You have absolutely nothing I want. I've come here to talk to you. Man, to fucking bastard. In the event you don't get it, you're the fucking bastard." Howie said he thought he had it all wrong. "I don't care. I'm here to tell you what I know of the day you killed your son and his family. Also, what you're going to be going to prison for. If you manage in some way to get out of going to prison, I'm going to kill you."

"Just like that. You're going to just up and kill me." Dwayne told him it was what he'd wanted to do since the first time he'd heard his name. "Well, ain't you just about the rudest person I've ever met? Other than that bitch of a wife of my son's. I told him not to marry her. Begged him not to breed with her too. Then he had those mongrels by her, and I had to set things to right."

"By killing innocent children and the woman that loved them? You're ten times worse than any of us thought you were." Howie said he was practical. "You're a fucking murderer is what you are."

"You say tomato, and I say tomato." He'd pronounced them the same way. Dwayne didn't even bother correcting him. Letting it go, he asked him what he was going to do now. "Nothing that I don't want to. That would include me going to prison. There is some insurance money that I'm going to collect on now that they're all dead and their bodies have been released. Thank you for taking care that they're buried for me. Right nice of your family. Also, the house they lived in is being updated for me to live in. I have all kinds of plans, so you know."

"I'd not make too many of them if I were you. The insurance money isn't going to be paid out. A number of reasons for that, but the main one is that you can't collect on insurance when you kill someone for it. Not to mention, the waiting period for you to have the insurance and when the person is murdered wasn't nearly long enough."

"Minor details. Nothing I can't put up a stink about and still be able to collect on. As for me murdering my family, I got to thinking on that when your brother hurt me. By the way, I think the courts aren't going to be none too happy with that either. Finding out that one of their citizens has hurt me. Not a good thing to have happen to a grieving man. Anyway, you've no proof at all that I did a thing. Your brother mentioned the gun—not true. I got to thinking about that, and I did leave the gun there. Just as I thought I had. As for where he was sitting, I'm going to just say that he was mighty depressed, and since he could sit in that seat without any trouble from the bitch, then that'll fly too. Again, a grieving man sort of thing."

"So you do admit to killing your son and his family." Howie said he wasn't admitting anything right now. He wasn't going to either since he was portraying a man who lost his family. "I see. You don't want to take credit for killing your own family because it might make you look bad. You go on thinking you're going to get away with it. Not that I care. Either way, you're going to be dead soon. Did whoever told you about your arm tell you that you're going to have to be careful about blood clots forever? That as of the moment you squirted that glue into your open wound, you left yourself open for all kinds of trouble?"

"I have money enough that I can take care I have a clean bill of health. Even if I have to find me someone to change me into something else, then I'll be around for a long time. With everything in working order, too." He asked him if he meant his arm. "Yes. I'm not a stupid man. I know just what being changed can do. Why, if I was hurt in my nut sack, I'd be healed in no time."

"You think you can grow back your arm?" Howie nodded. Dwayne couldn't help it. He burst out laughing. "It doesn't work that way unless you had the ability to be able to grow back your appendages before. You couldn't, could you? I'm thinking you didn't have it. Otherwise, you would have taken care of that already. And speaking of not being caught for the murder of your son, you left your prints all over the storage unit they died in. There was enough DNA in that thing that it might have been thought you'd died in there with them. Also, on the car that was used to pump the poison into it. Then there are the bullets you used. Howard's prints weren't on them. Just yours."

"Bullshit. I wore gloves. Not only that, but you got no proof I took them into that container either. I was careful." Dwayne asked him if he'd been wrapped up in plastic from head to toe. "No. I didn't need to do that. Could say I hugged them."

"Not going to fly, I'm afraid. You see, I have it on good authority that you've never hugged the children. Howard's wife either." He asked him how he knew that. "I've spoken to them. Your daughter-in-law, Bree, told us. And the police. She even told them of the camera she had in the house that she'd never told you about. As well as the one that was in the car when you put them in it."

"No fucking way. There wasn't any power to the car. There isn't any way that it would have recorded me doing anything." Dwayne was enjoying this a great deal more than he thought he should be. He asked him if he remembered seeing the solar panels on the roof of the car. "You lie."

"Am I? No, I'm not. Also, there wasn't any carbon in their lungs. Not any of them. The test results came back this afternoon. Not only were your prints on the shell casings of the ammo, but also, I'm pleased to tell you that you sweated on the bullets when you were working on them. There was enough DNA on those to convict even a dead man when they tested them." Dwayne threw back his blanket, and Howie stared at his leg—or at least where his leg had been. "Oh, by the way. I asked that they didn't tell you that three days ago, they had to remove a great part of your leg. Blood clots got into your system. Keeping you under until I could get the evidence about the murders you committed was something the police had done. Good luck with prison, Howie. Inmates, even ones that murder, do not care for a child being killed."

The police came into the room just as Dwayne stood up. As Howie was read his rights, Dwayne left the room in favor of getting some fresh air. Air that didn't smell like the murderer he'd been asked to see if he could get him to confess. Making his way home now that he was in his car, it was Matthew that contacted him about the recording devices.

I have it all on thumb drives for you to have a copy of for yourself. Not that I think anyone is going to be questioning your word against his on this, but you never know. Dwayne asked him if there was anything else he needed to know. *Not that I can think of. The kids did want to have you around for dinner one night. Pizza hot from the delivery guy is what has become their favorite. Kids. They're very strange, aren't they?*

They are at that. I'm hoping to have a couple more of them myself someday. Matthew told him he'd love every second of it. *Thank you. I believe I will. Having Jamie as a son, it's certainly made me think that having them isn't as bad as I had thought it would be. I remember us as kids and how much we hid from our parents.*

I'm betting everything I have that not only do your parents know about it, but they're waiting for you to have children of your own so they can tell them about it. It's what all parents do to their kids. They both laughed hard on that, Dwayne agreeing that his parents more than likely did know it all. *I wanted to ask you a favor. It's not a big deal, but I was wondering if you could ask Raven to pay me less.*

I know she'll tell me, no, but I have more than I can spend right now.

No, I won't do that. You deserve whatever she's paying you. More, I think. He said he was making a great deal. *You'll need it when the kids go off to college. Not to mention all those pizzas delivered to your home. If you want me to talk to Raven, I want you to know I'll ask her to pay you more, not less. You've helped me and the police – hell, the country – more than we can ever repay you for.*

All right. I won't mention it again. But I have to tell you, it was my pleasure to do this for this family. You took me under your wings when I needed it most and helped me in ways that no one has ever helped me before. Dwayne told him it was his pleasure to do that for him and his kids. *Thanks. All right. I'll let you go. You have a nice evening, Dwayne. Enjoy life. I know I am.*

He called Brit to tell her what had happened. She seemed distracted, so he asked her if she was all right. Dwayne nearly drove off the road when she answered him.

"I'm currently trying to put on a nightie that I got for you to see me in. I'm terrible at figuring it out, just so you know. Also, Jamie is at his grandparents', and we're all alone in the house." He asked her if she had plans for him.

"I do. I'm going to meet you at the door naked. I've only just decided it's too much effort for me to figure this sucker out when all you're going to do is rip it from me. I hope."

"The thought of you naked and waiting for me is making me hurt right now." She asked him if he was hard. "Unless you want to heal me when I have an accident, you should refrain from talking too much about how hard I am until I get there. Right now, I'm about to bust out of my pants. I'm so hard."

Her giggle nearly did him in. As he was pulling into the driveway, she giggled again. "You should know that I'm so wet right now I'm sure you're going to have to lick me to clean me up. And I want you to eat me so desperately it's all I can think about."

"Christ, woman." He put his phone away so he could get out of the car and to the house. As soon as he was through the door, she was in his arms, her legs wrapped around his body. "You're going to have to slow down, love. You're going to have your enjoyment long before I get to be the one that gives it to you."

"I need to come. Help me before I combust, Dwayne. Please help me." He pushed her against the wall, her legs dropping automatically. As soon as she was steady on her feet, he buried his mouth over her creamy pussy. "Yes."

Her scream hurt his ears, but it was the most satisfying sound he'd heard. Even her fingers yanking his hair painfully was something he'd gladly endure over and over for her. Making her come, tasting her richness, was a joy to him.

She came again and again. Her body trembled for him, and him alone. Even as she begged him to stop, to give her his body, Dwayne couldn't have stopped no matter how much she begged.

Feeling her yanking his hair again, he looked up at her. "You look so good. So beautiful right now." He kissed her thigh, then her belly.

"Take me, Dwayne. I want to feel your cock inside of me. Now. I want you now."

Standing up, he picked her up, but not before kissing her, tasting a bit of blood where she'd bitten her lip. Taking her up the stairs, there were a couple of times when he was sure they weren't going to make it, that they were going to end up making love right there on the stairs. Then they were finally in their room, the room that Brit had been sleeping in since she'd moved into the house.

Putting her on the floor again, the bed

seemed so far away when he made his way across to it. Their bodies were touching while he backed her to their goal. Dwayne couldn't seem to get enough of her. Not just touching her but tasting her as well.

Brit's skin tasted sweet and spicy. Her blood tasted like peppers his mom had grown when he was a child. Even when her legs touched the bed, he picked her up above his head enough that he could lick her navel. Laying her on the bed, he stood over her, his cock straining in a way that he'd never experienced before.

"I'd love to suck on your cock for you. But not this time." He felt his disappointment all the way to his feet. "Now, I want you inside of me. Taking me to higher peaks than you have already. Then, if I don't kill us both with my need, I'll take you so far down my throat that you're going to come hard."

"I'm thinking you're very close to doing that now—killing me, I mean. I've never enjoyed myself as much as I am with you." She grinned as she sat up with her elbows beneath her. "If I could paint, I'd most assuredly paint you as you are right now. Sexy and relaxed. Your hair messy like it is. Your lips swollen from my mouth. I love you, Brit. More than I ever thought it was possible to love a woman."

"I love you. Loving you came to me so easily and unexpectedly. It was nothing I ever thought I'd feel, not with any man—not with you." He lay down beside her, his body flush with hers chest to breast. "You're the most perfect specimen of a man. It'll be hard for me to look at you after this, knowing what sort of body you're hiding under that suit you wear."

Pulling her to his mouth, he kissed her, giving her not just his passion for her but his love for her as well. He knew when the magic came over her. Not hard and fast as he thought it would, but a gentle sort of soothing blend of what he'd already given her and what she had now. It was perfect. Her not being in pain made him feel wonderfully amazing.

Looking at her when he pulled away, Dwayne asked her to marry him. "I'll make you happy. Never harm you or our son. I love him as well. I'd love to adopt him into my family because he already has a very special place in our hearts." She said he'd have to talk to him about that. "I can do that. Now, however, I want to make love with you. Touch you in ways that I've not before. Taste the bits of your flesh that I've missed. Will you marry me?"

"Again, you'll have to ask Jamie. We come as a family, and we will make that decision as a family. All right?" He rolled her to her back, wrapping her legs around his hips as he did. Sliding into her, Dwayne felt amazingly complete. As if not only had he found his mate in Brit, but he'd found a soulmate as well. He couldn't be any happier than he was at this very moment.

They made love then, slowly, touching again, kissing each other. When they came, this time together, Dwayne cried out his release as he filled her with himself. Her sheath wrapped tightly around his cock, Dwayne came with her. Falling asleep in her arms, holding her to him, he thought there was nothing in the world he couldn't conquer with her by his side. Love was a strange thing, he realized. It gave him a peace he'd not felt since he was a child. Peace and love were forever his.

Chapter 6

Mr. Shelby—Carl, as he told her to call him—was working out better than she could have imagined. Dwayne was happy too that the older man had sold his company outright to Addington and was now solely making Brit's things work for her to rent. He was home at night, happy as he'd ever been, and Carl finally was able to put money in the bank for him and his wife to have some time together on vacations and such.

Answering the phone, Brit was surprised to hear back from one of her clients so soon after posting on her page that she had working items now.

"I'm so glad to hear that, my dear. I have an upcoming project I was having some trouble finding things for. You couldn't have had better timing for me." He gave her a list of things he needed and how many. "Also, if you ever decide on cars—they don't have to work for what I have in mind for them—those will be a hit for us too. In fact, I know of a man that is going to sell off his stock as soon as this week. You buy some of it, and I'll rent as many as I can from you. That's a deal you can take to the bank. You've always been a fair-minded person on rentals, and never have you gotten out of joint with me when I'm a few days late. A person in my business appreciates that. Thank you."

"Thank you. I'll look now to see what I can figure out about the sale." He said he'd send her the link. As soon as she got it, Brit knew she really was going to have a hit on her hands. Now, if she could somehow get some upfront money for it, she thought with a laugh. "I'll get back to you on this to let you know if I am successful in buying anything. Thank you again for the order, too."

She knew that Dwayne was working on a deal this morning but didn't want to wait on getting his approval for her to use as much money as she thought she'd need to. Looking over the cars as well as the going prices, she was shocked to see there was very little in the way of bids on any of the cars. She thought she could buy the entire lot of cars, all three hundred of them, for little to nothing. After getting the total price on what was being asked, she called Holly.

"I'm with Raven if you don't mind me bringing her along." She said it was a business deal she was looking to make, and she didn't have enough ready cash to do it. "Well then, you want Raven there too. She has a head for this sort of thing. We're nearly pulling into your drive right now, love. See you in a few. Oh, could you see if there are any of those pretty little cakes your cook makes? I so love them."

She said she'd ask. As she was going to the kitchen, Jamie came downstairs just as the front door was being answered. There was Holly, Raven, and her two babies. She told them that Molly was on a retreat for her class projects that were due in a few days.

"I'm going to have to change them, then feed them. Can you help me, Jamie? I'd pay you." He told her he enjoyed the kids, he called them and appreciated her asking him rather than shoving them into his arms. They laughed as Raven went into her office and sat on the floor to change her son's diaper. "Tell me what you have going, Brit, and I'll tell you what I think about it. Then I fully expect you to do what you want anyway. I'm not nearly as brilliant as my grandma thinks I am."

After explaining what she had in the works now and how Carl was fixing things, so they worked, Brit went on to explain the cars and the auction that was going on right now.

"They're going for about half the price I think they should. I've asked too, and I can get back nearly the total amount for the cars on just one rental." She asked if that was a lot. "A car, I was told, could go for as much as eight thousand a month for a rental. Triple that if they plan on destroying them. Though I won't let that be a part of the deal unless I find myself having more than one of the same model."

"And these cars you're thinking of buying. How much are you willing to pay for them?" After telling her what she thought she could get away with, Raven said she was impressed. "While I never gave it a thought on where they get the cars they have in movies, I can see where this would be a very lucrative money maker. I can help you out. I'd be happy to do that for you."

"I'll pay you back. With interest." She asked her why she'd not contacted Dwayne.

"He's in a meeting all day with two business deals that he wants to make work. I promised I'd not bother him unless it was an emergency."

"Call him." Brit told Holly she didn't want to bother him. "Call him. That way, he can walk away from the people I have him talking to, and they can talk about it. Call his office so the deal will go better. Not that I don't think Raven can help you with this, but you need to talk it over with Dwayne. I know he's good for the money, too."

Picking up the phone, Brit called his office. She was glad when his secretary answered. After telling her that she wanted to talk to Dwayne but at his desk, she laughed, telling her that he might need it about now. Apparently, it wasn't going well for the business he was supposed to be talking to.

"What are they doing that has you so frustrated?" Dwayne laughed and told her they were breathing. Holly asked for him to be on speaker. "Okay, when you're finished, I have something I need to talk to you about too."

"All right, love. Holly, Mr. Dillon is a no-nonsense man that I actually like. However, his son is an ass that needs to get his head on straight before he wheels and deals his father into the poor house." She asked him what was going on. "His son wants to expand the business by double. There isn't the need for it. They get what they have orders for out in a timely, well-spaced timeframe. Then there is the fact that the employees are happy and working well. Not only that, but his business has taken a downturn since his son, who I think is sabotaging the company with his attitude, has been helping around the plant. And by helping, I mean he's been telling the employees he's going to be in charge soon, and there are going to be cutbacks. I would love to tell his father that, but I don't want bloodshed in my office."

"Do you think it would be all right if I spoke to him? Tell him he has a phone call from…I don't know, his wife." He said he could do that and set him up in an office for it. "All right, Dwayne. Good job on this. I'll talk to him. You tell me what you'd like to see happen, and I'll make it work."

"I'd like for him to sell shares of the business to his employees. That way, they can have a say in who replaces Mr. Dillon when the time comes. If anyone knows the business the best, it would be them." Holly asked him how that would work. "They'd take a small cut in pay to be able to pay for their portion of whatever he's willing to give them. I think he'd be better off selling them at least seventy-five percent. That way, he makes a profit, and they do as well. Profit shares would be paid quarterly. That would be, if all of them wanted in on it, about five grand a quarter, for each of the fifteen people that work there. Like I said, the business is doing well, but not enough to expand. If they expand, believe it or not, they'll not be able to hire anyone to work the extra area. That will cause trouble with them when they have to do twice the work in a much larger area."

When he had it set up for Holly to call the man, Dwayne asked Brit what she needed. She told him everything that was going on. The profit that she could make off one rental, as well as how much things were going for right now. The auction would end in an hour, she told him.

"How much total if you were to bid highest on all of the cars?" She told him what she'd figured out. "See, I knew you'd have that number too. We're going to do well together. Put in a higher bid on all the cars. I can see you're going to need a larger warehouse. I have just the property for it."

"I've not won yet, you know." He told her

he had faith in her. "I'm glad. Okay, can you wait on me to do it? I know you're busy."

"Margaret has just gotten Mr. Dillon into the other office, and I don't want to spend any more time than I have to with his son. So this is perfect." He asked her if she was putting in the bids. "I know you're going to do this. I think it's a perfect investment for us. But you didn't have to call me, Brit. If you think it will be a good thing to put money into, then I'm all for it as well. You know your business better than I do."

"I know, but it could be a disaster too." Dwayne told her he doubted it. "You have more faith in me than I do."

Winning the first car, she was happy with that. If she won the rest, that would be something she'd deal with as they won. Right now, she was dancing around the office talking to Jamie and Raven about it.

"There are twenty-eight cars and trucks. The one I'm most excited for is the nineteen twenty-two Ford Huckster. I have pictures of my grandma sitting in one as a teenager." When they were halfway through the list, she was winning them all. Calculating how much she had spent, she started figuring out how she was going to get them here. Some were drivable, but others were not. Then it occurred to her to see where the cars were. "You're not going to believe this, but all the cars are on a single lot about an hour from here. I should have checked that before I started bidding."

Dwayne laughed. "I have to get back now. Mr. Dillon is headed back into the conference room with a little pep in his step. You let me know about the cars, honey. I want to know how you're doing on each car. Even if you say you've won and leave it at that for me."

After hanging up, she watched the rest of the cars going her way. When they were down to the last two, she was outbid on both of them. Brit was willing to go more on them since she'd gotten such a good deal on all the others.

"Can you go up on your own, or do they have a set price?" She said it was a set amount. Sippy had shown up about ten minutes ago and was watching the sale over her shoulder. "Go up to that amount, but add a buck to it. That's what I do sometimes."

After putting in her next bid on them, she watched as the clock counted down on the sale. With these two, if she won them, she was going to make all her money back on a single rental, not including the buyer's premium and the cost of the new building. Brit not only won the last two cars, but she got them for the dollar more that Sippy had told her. Reaching out to Dwayne, she told him she'd gotten them all.

This calls for a celebration. My deal went through as well. Not only that, but Mr. Dillon is going to sell the seventy-five percent to his workers, and he's fired his son. Whatever Holly said to him, it worked. This is just what I needed. You and I are both winners in our day. She told him she was going to make arrangements to get the cars here. She had thirty days. *Good. Long enough for us to get a building up and working. We'll take a trip to the lot and take some pictures of your new rentals so you can put them on your website. I love you, my dear. This is just what I wanted to hear.*

She made arrangements to have the building put on the property Dwayne had told her about. Paying a little extra wasn't necessary, as it was a downtime for the company, and they were more than willing to get it done on time for her. They would also hire some of the pack to work on it. A good day for everyone.

When Dwayne showed up a little after five, she and Jamie were ready to go. He'd gotten Raven to get them reservations at one of the nicer places in Columbus, and they were going to spend the night at a hotel and go to the zoo the next day. Since it was Saturday, they were going to enjoy whatever came their way.

The restaurant was very posh. As they were being seated, Mr. Dillon came over to talk to them. He said he and his wife were celebrating as well. Their son, Parker, had moved out today.

"He was too old to be there anyway. I was happy when he said he was too upset to live at home anymore and was going to move out. I think when he left, he thought we'd be begging him to stay, but neither of us said a word." Jamie asked if they'd changed the locks. "We did. We really did. Most fun I've had in a good long time. And I have Addington to thank for it. And especially you, young man. You saved me a lot of heartache with this."

"It was my pleasure." He asked the older couple to join them, and they agreed readily. Brit didn't mind—she was just happy they were having a good day too. "No business at the table now. I'd like it to be just two families celebrating life."

"I couldn't agree more. No, I can't." Dinner was fun. They ordered appetizers for the table and shared them with each other. Jamie had fun, too, trying things he'd never had before. When the check came, Mr. Dillon insisted on paying for their meal. "It's the least I can do after you asking us to join you. I don't think I've had a more enjoyable meal in a long time."

"We've enjoyed it too."

They were leaving when Mr. Dillon asked what they were planning tomorrow. He had a business deal he wanted to go over with him. Before he could tell him they had plans already, his wife spoke up.

"Parker Dillon. You are not going to make them miss their trip to the zoo because you want to work on another project with this young family. You'll talk to him on Monday, on a workday." She kissed Dwayne on the cheek, as well as Brit and Jamie, thanking Jamie for telling her about his trip. "He'll work you like he works if you allow it. Weekends and after five are family time. No matter how good the deal is. Good night, all of you. He'll be calling you on Monday morning, eight sharp, and even then, he'll have been up for hours waiting for you to enter the office."

They were all laughing as they headed to their cars. As they were getting into the car to drive to the hotel, Jamie asked if they could find a place to get some ice cream. Instead of driving to the place, they walked there, and each of them got a cone the size of their heads as they continued window shopping along the busy streets.

~*~

"Hi." Brit looked up from her computer when Sasha spoke, telling her she was sorry but didn't hear her come in. "You were buried up to your ass in whatever you're doing. I know that because you kept saying that over and over. Did you fire her yet? I would."

"My inventory control person, Sara. Yes, I fired her. She wasn't using the program to take things out of inventory, so a few things were double rented. I paid a great deal of money for that program and then had Matthew tweak it for me. And I want people to use it." Sasha asked if Matthew had tweaked it or rewritten it. "He started out just tweaking it. Then he told me I was better off starting from scratch. The one I had wasn't accounting for the inventory I had coming in unless I put it in manually. But I'm sure you didn't come here to talk to me about that."

"I didn't. Your sister is here with us. She has a favor to ask you. By the way, I don't know if you heard or not, but Howie is going to be in a hospital setting in prison until his hearing.

He's caused some trouble at the local hospital, so much that they've asked to have him moved." She asked if her sister needed her to hurt Howie. "No. Nothing like that. She and the others will take care of him once he's on the other side. Their side. But the favor is a big one. Bree has been visiting places around town that she's helping. The soup kitchen is one of the places she's gone to and done a little moving things around. Also, the veteran's hospital in Cleveland. Bree is having a lot of fun, she told me."

"What's the favor? Does she want me to volunteer there too? I'd do just about anything for her right now." Sasha said it was nothing like that. Not yet. "Then tell me. She's my sister, and I miss her. Whatever she needs, I'm there for her."

"She would like you to fund the local nursing home to have someone come in and have activities for them. That's not what she came to me about, but that is a good idea. They have the crafts there, but no one to lead them to do things. They're bored, she thinks." Brit made notes on the things Sasha told her about. "There is also an opening for a cook there. She said you know someone that would fit perfectly for them."

"Mr. Caldwell." Sasha said that was him. "Yes, I just spoke to him a couple of days ago.

He's looking for a place to lay his hat. I wonder if they'd allow him to live there while he cooks for them. He doesn't really need the money, but if they could give him space to work and to live, he'd be happy to help out there."

"Bree said she'd nudge the right people for him to have that." Sasha looked in the direction of the bookshelf. Brit waited. Whatever her sister was saying to the other woman, she was liking it. "Your sister is brilliant, by the way. I love her way of thinking outside the box with things. All right. She said there is a building in the downtown area that would be perfect to put on plays. For the elderly to come and watch, she told me. Her way of thinking is that children can put on plays for them, then have a nice lunch with the residents at the nursing home."

"I have a list of buildings we already own. Where is it?" Sasha gave her the address, and she was disappointed to see that Raven and Sawyer owned it. "They'll get to do this and not me."

"Not necessarily. If you go to Raven about it, she'll be pissy about you getting in first on the deal. I'm betting, knowing her, that she'll donate the building to the nursing home so they can use it for all kinds of things like the one Bree wants." Making her notes, she knew just what she was going to name it too if she was allowed. "Bree said for you not to name it for her. That she'd rather you called it The Jerry and Robin Theater. I love the sound of that. And the last name associated with Howie won't going to be on it either. A win-win, I think."

"I love that idea. This way, we can honor those two lovely children and not have Howie's name on it at all. Yes, I'll talk to Raven."

Raven came into the room and asked her what she was going to ask her. She told her what her sister wanted to happen.

"Damn it. Can I not have a good idea anymore? Of course, I'll help you. But I'm pissy I didn't get to do it first."

They were all three laughing when Brit asked if her sister was still there.

"No. She left." There was more to it, but Sasha didn't elaborate. Brit didn't ask either. Whatever her sister had done, it was for a later conversation. "There is nothing wrong with your sister leaving, Brit. She can't stay here for long periods of time. I promise you, it's just that she left. Silly woman. If there was something more, I would tell you. However, the building is in your name, Raven. What is it you have to do to deed it to the nursing home? Or will you do that?"

"Not if I can help it. If I sign it over to them, it will cost us both in higher taxes. What I'm hoping they agree to is for the building to stay in the Addington company, and I'll donate the time they use it to them. That way, there isn't such a hit to the nursing home to own it, and I can deduct the use of it from my taxes. I wouldn't usually do that, but since the nursing home is not for profit, I have to make it work for both of us." Brit knew about taxes and how to get around them taking everything you owned. "I'm sure you have a name for it already. And I'm going to be pissed off about it as well, aren't I?"

"More than likely. The name is The Jerry and Robin Theater. I love it." Raven pouted, but it looked good on her. "Not my idea. None of it. My sister has been looking around and figured it out. So both of us are out."

They played around with the things they'd need for the building for several hours after that. Occasionally she'd get back to her inventory issue, but it was nothing pressing. The things being double rented had fixed themselves over the course of the day, and she was happy. However, now she had to hire two people to work the computers instead of just the one replacement.

Since the cars were big-ticket items, she decided they had to have one person devoted to not just the rental of them but also keeping track of the inventory. Since being with Dwayne, she no longer let anyone collect the money for their projects but handled that herself. Even payroll, which was much easier than the company she'd hired to do it for her, had told her. Matthew, who was becoming an invaluable part of her business, had set up a program for her that would not just read the time clock that was now digital but would calculate what the people made weekly. It was a piece of cake after that.

"Jamie's been working for me. Did he tell you that?" Brit told Raven he had said he was working for some pocket money. "I hope I'm paying him better than that. He's become handy in making sure the clothing I'm selling is priced the way I want it, as well as doing spell checks on the descriptions. I was amazed at how many he found on just the first page of dresses. I hope you know how smart that kid is."

"I do. Since he was in preschool, they told me he was better at figuring out things than the other students. Then when he started first grade, they were giving him work for sixth grade and upwards. I was a hold-out on having him advance until he was at a better age to be able to handle it. When he came home the first day after being put in high school at nine, he thanked me for that."

"I bet he did." Sippy was having a cupcake that was forever around now that she knew she couldn't gain an ounce. "I homeschooled my boys up until they were ready. Then they skipped right over high school and were in college by the time they were just about ready to go into what would have been fifth grade for them, had they been in school all along."

"Sawyer is hoping our kids aren't that advanced. He said he did miss a great deal by having his high school graduation at twelve." Brit laughed when Sippy got huffy with Raven. "He is glad he was able to do that, but he says he'd not been able to go on school trips and other things without a parent. I guess the first time he took his dad on one of the trips, he barely lived it down."

"I remember that. Saul came home really upset about the way they'd treated Sawyer. They called him a daddy's boy that couldn't go to the bathroom without his daddy around. Things only a child would say to another one." Sippy smiled then. "He showed them. Graduating at the top of his class at so young of an age has been talked about for years. My boys are brilliant, the same as my grandchildren."

Brit thought Sippy was about the best grandma in the world. She doted on the kids when they were around and never treated them differently if they were adopted or not. Holly did the same with her great-grandchildren. Next summer, she was taking Jamie on a cruise with her and Molly, simply because he told her he'd never been on one.

"Did I tell you about the money?" She knew she'd interrupted them when they were speaking. Telling them she was sorry, she said it had only just popped into her head. "Gunner came by to ask me about some of the projects I have going. He figured with that money he found in the desk he'd gotten, I could help him with a couple of projects. Gunner and Andi were all for the idea of putting an addition on the food pantry building. Andi was telling me she and Gunner were using the money for good and to put Mr. Henderson's name on it so his children will know. He told me how the man's children hadn't even gone to his funeral. They weren't there for the sole reason that they thought he was broke."

"Have you seen the desk? It's beautiful. And perfect for Gunner. Andi did a wonderful job in having his medals framed and put in the room. You should go see it." Brit told Sippy she would. "So it's going to be called Henderson. I love that. The building has just been called the pantry or the food store since I've been around. I'm glad it's getting a good solid name now."

There were other projects they talked about. Most of them had been started and were finally being used. Brit was going to try and do more for the people around this town so she could feel good about living here. She also decided she was going to hire the people she needed locally so she could stimulate the economy some too.

"I saw your building the other day. It took me a while to figure out why you were having it put in with temperature control. Then I realized that with the weather around here, things like that could get wet and rot. Then they'd be no good to you." Brit told Penny, who had shown up a little while into their talk that she was also going to have a building put in for her other rentals. "I would imagine you have a great deal of inventory to move."

"I'm not going to move it all at once. I've

decided I'll have the renters move it for me. Each time something is returned, I'll have it brought here instead of back to New York. Also, I'll have time to build places where I can sort and store things." Penny asked her where she got her inventory. "You'd be surprised how much is easy and cheap to pick up at garage sales. Auctions too, but I get better prices when the people selling things they just want out of their home and sell it accordingly. The other day I got an entire living room set from the early sixties for twenty-five bucks. I'm in heavy with that one. Even after having it cleaned, it's still going to be very profitable."

"How do you know what to get? I mean, there wouldn't be much demand for some of it, would there?" Brit said it was all in demand, as there were movies being made all the time. "I guess that's right. When the movie comes out that you're a part of, I'd like to go with you to see it. So you can tell me what you were able to supply them with."

"I usually get premiere tickets to go. I've never used them before. I'll make sure I tell you when I get them from now on. It might be a lot of fun."

They were still having fun when Dwayne

came home from work. The women scattered quickly after that. It was nice to have some time with Dwayne after a long day of working. Even Jamie enjoyed it.

Chapter 7

Quincey moved to the middle of the pack. He supposed it was rude of him to call people, mostly humans, a pack, but to his way of thinking, saying it out loud and thinking it were two different things. Thinking things about people was what got him through the worst kind of patients. The light that told them when to walk was still red, but something just wasn't right about the man and woman in front of him.

He could tell they weren't together if the glares the man was giving the woman were any indication. Not to mention, he told her several times to get out of his space. Not that it did him any good—she never moved out of her place right behind him.

Quincey saw the big truck coming down

the road. It had been the safest and the quickest construction route for the new building going in on one of the properties they all owned. Even as he was thinking this was going to end badly, the man moved. Then the woman did.

Grabbing her back from following the man, he was driven to the sidewalk by her turning on him. Leaping up, he grabbed her again and buried her face into his chest to keep her from the horrors of what had just happened. She was still fighting for freedom as everyone around them backed from the dead man's body and the truck that had ended his life.

"I have you." She fought free of him and then began signing at him. Putting his hands over hers, he stopped her, but only long enough for him to sign back to her that she needed to slow down. "It's been a while. I'm a little rusty. I didn't want you to follow the man into moving traffic."

She turned then, looking where the rest of the people were looking. When she turned back to him, she thanked him as only a deaf person could. Her fingers to her chin, then pointing them toward him. Having her settled, he went to the man lying broken on the road. Even though he could see that his back was broken, as was his neck, Quincey tried his pulse on what was left of his throat. He was able to pronounce him dead. He then reached for his brother.

There's been an accident/suicide on Main Street, Sawyer. Could you please send help? He asked if anyone else was hurt. *No. Just the man. The truck driver couldn't have stopped in time if he had seen the man. Whoever he was, he timed it perfectly to step in front of the truck and end his life.*

I'm on my way. I've called an ambulance too. He thanked his brother. *You were there, I'm assuming. Are you sure he wasn't pushed?*

Positive. There is a deaf woman here too. I managed to keep her from moving into the same accident. I think she was using him as a reference as to when she could cross the street.

The woman was upset—anyone within two inches of her could tell that. Going to her, Quincey was careful to wipe the man's blood from his hand as he got closer. He didn't want to frighten her any more than she already was. When she looked up at him, he could also see fear there. Assuring her that she wasn't going to be in trouble had her smacking his forehead.

"You're very violent, aren't you?" She told him to fuck off. "Rude. I was just going to let you know that the police are on their way and that my brother knows you weren't involved."

Quincey had to think about some of the words he was signing to her, and when she laughed, not a sound moving past her upturned mouth, he grinned back at her. He explained to her that he hadn't used ASL for a while.

"I had no idea he was going to get hurt when he moved." Quincey explained to her that he thought the man had committed suicide. And had she followed him, she would have been killed too. "I can't hear the clicking. There were too many people for me to see the other side, or this one, to tell me when I could walk."

"You're fine now, so that's all that matters, right?" She nodded and looked to his right. Turning that way as well, he saw Sawyer get out of his truck and walk toward him. "That's my older brother. He's the acting sheriff here until they find someone to replace him. He knows ASL too."

ASL, or the American Sign Language, had been something he'd been taught by his mom. All of them had been when she homeschooled them. Mom had learned it from her aunt, who was born deaf. It had, over the years, come in handy when he had to speak to someone that couldn't hear.

Sawyer seemed to be doing all right now that he'd told her that he too was a little rusty, so Quincey started away. When his hand was grabbed, he turned back to the woman and said he wasn't going to leave her. He needed to talk to the coroner.

"Her name is Beth Stone. She's new here in town to teach ASL to the staff at the hospital. Did you know anything about that?" He told Sawyer he no longer read the emails at the hospital, as they were stupid. "Be that as it may, could you check on it for me? Not that I don't believe her, but she has literally only just arrived and hasn't had a chance to figure out where they're putting her while here."

"Yes, I can do that." Pulling out his cell phone, it didn't bother him in the least that Beth was still holding onto him. Asking for the department that scheduled classes for the staff, he wasn't just told about the woman, Beth, but was also told that she was late. "She's been involved in an accident. She's not injured or a part of it, but she was a witness to it."

"Is this the body that is coming to us soon, Doctor Bishop?" He told her he'd pronounced him dead at the scene and that he would be in later to sign the death certificate for him.

"Thank you, sir. I'll make sure I tell the others what has happened to her. Also, if you'd not mind, when you come, I'd like you to take her housing information so she may have it. I'm to understand she's deaf."

"Yes, she is." There wasn't anything more that he wanted to add to the conversation, so he closed his phone. Turning to Sawyer, he found himself alone again with Beth. She asked him what was going on. He explained to her what was happening with the hospital.

"Thank you. To be honest with you, I'd forgotten about getting in touch with them." She looked at her hand on his shirt but only released him long enough to sign. "You must think I'm a loony, holding you like this. But it anchors me."

"I don't think that at all. You've had something traumatic happen near you, and it's understandable that you're upset and need to anchor yourself." Something occurred to him in that moment, and he felt his heart rate pick up. "Beth, are you seeing anyone? Married or something like that? I mean, do you have someone in your life right now?"

"Why? Has someone contacted you? I'm not going to go to my mom. She isn't a nice person. Did she have someone contact you to get in touch with me?" He said he didn't know who she was, but no, no one had. "Then why do you care if I'm with someone or not?"

"I'm a shifter. White Bengal tiger. Do you know anything about shifters?" She said she knew a great many shifters, but sadly, no tigers. "Yes, well, I'd have to figure it out, but I'm thinking the reason you feel so comfortable around me, and me you, is that you might be my mate. I'd have to get closer to you to find out."

"How close?" He told her. "All right. You can sniff me. But nothing else. I know you won't hurt me, or you would have already, but just don't get too fresh with me."

Burying his nose into her neck, he knew immediately that she wasn't his mate, but she had been around someone that might be. Instead of asking her who it was, he just told her she wasn't, but that he was here for her.

"I thank you for that. I know a few shifters, as I said. And a man that is a wolf nearly married the wrong woman when it was her mother all the time he was smelling on her. He didn't realize it until the day of the wedding." He told Beth that was something he'd been thinking too. Then asked her if she had anyone. "My mother. But you'd better hope it's not her. She's off her rocker. Mom is in an asylum for the criminally insane. Mom killed my dad, sister, and brother, and a bunch of other people one night. It was much more than her putting a bullet in their heads, she— Well, that's one you'll have to look up on your own. Melody Stone. Five years ago."

"I'll look into that. No one else then?" She smiled at him and told him she had two sisters, one younger, the other older. "I'm assuming they don't live around here. If not, then I don't think it could be them. This person you would have had contact with recently."

"Both of them do, as a matter of fact." He smiled at her and said he might be better off letting it go. "Doubtful you could survive that, Doctor Bishop."

"Doubtful that either one of them would want to attach themselves to a country doctor with no chance of moving on to something more. Not that I want that, but I'm not all that much where a woman would fall over herself for me."

She told him to behave, then the police asked to speak to her. Since Sawyer was working for the department, he let him take care of translating for her. However, he didn't leave her side. She needed protection as much as his tiger did, he thought. She was tough and seemed to be able to defend herself. Watching her as she answered their questions, he thought about her family as he looked it up on his phone.

Melody Stone had made the front page in every newspaper around the world, it looked like. She'd killed not only two of her children, but her husband, his mother, sister, brother, as well as a mailman, two men who picked up the trash, and as two officers when they had tried to arrest her. Melody had, according to the report he was reading, just simply snapped one day.

After reading the accounting of what had happened to the people she had killed in her home, Quincey shivered. The only reason Beth and Joanie had been able to live was that they'd hidden in the basement. Hearing the screams of their mother's victims, as well as the laughter from her the entire three days they'd been trapped with no way out, had been a lot to endure, the author of the article had written.

Just as he was finishing the article, he was touched on the arm by someone. Looking at Beth, he asked her if she was all right. She asked him to call her sisters and that she'd buy him lunch.

"I'll call them for you, but you don't have to buy me lunch, Beth. I was joking when I said I was nothing but a country doctor. I have other means of making money." She said she figured that but still wanted to have lunch with him. "All right. But I'll buy. It's a manly thing to do."

The place across the street from his office served a really good French dip sandwich. He ordered that, as well as a cup of their vegetable soup to go with it. Beth wanted the same, but instead of water, she wanted tea. Writing down the numbers after the server left, Quincey wondered what he was getting himself into. As soon as the phone was answered by someone cursing, he knew this person was going to be his mate.

"My name is Quincey Bishop. I was—" She told him she didn't know him. "I'm aware of that, Ms. Stone, but your sister is here with me, and she's—"

"Is she hurt? I told her to take one of us with her. Damn it. Did you hurt her?" He said he'd not. "Well? What the hell are you doing with my little sister then? I'm telling you right now, you're not going to get away with—"

"Will you calm the fuck down for a minute and let me finish telling you the reason I called you?" No apology came from her end, but he was just pissy enough to let it go for now. "She was witness to an accident that claimed the life of a young man. She wasn't involved or injured, but she's understandably shook up. However, why she would think you'd be a comfort to her is beyond me. We're at the Dixie Restaurant on Main Street."

Closing the phone, he didn't want to tell Beth what had happened, but she asked, so he told her the one that had answered the phone was a rude bitch. Beth smiled and told him it could have been either of her sisters. Neither of them were good with people.

They ate their lunch and spoke about her job. He'd not been as excited about his job as she was about hers in a long time, he realized. Of course, she was just beginning hers, and he'd been a doctor for nearly eight years. Christ, he thought, that was a long time.

When two women sat down with them, just barged into their lunch, he watched the conversation the two of them were having with Beth. They were pissed. Not at her, but that she'd not called them right away. Beth told them both to fuck off and that she was a grown woman. That got him laughing, and the two newcomers glared at him.

"You two are a great deal alike. I'm assuming you boss everyone around when you feel you're in the right." He spoke to the other two and signed for Beth to understand him. "I told you she was fine, yet there you are checking her out like she was some sort of kid you have to boss—" One of them told him it was none of us business. Quincey slammed his hands on the table and spoke again. "Stop interrupting me when I'm speaking. You've done that so many times I can only assume you're used to people letting you ride all over them. Well, I'm not going to allow you to beat up on her or me. So you can either calm the fuck down, or you can just get the hell out of here. Beth and I were having a nice lunch until you two arrived."

Neither of them said another word to him or Beth. When the server arrived, he asked them if they needed a menu. They both agreed to have whatever Beth was having. When the server walked away, he knew the woman talking was the one who had answered the phone.

"I'm sorry. I'm not good around people. My name is Grace. My sister is Joanie. You've been really nice by taking care of Beth, so she wasn't too traumatized, and we all appreciate that." He told Grace it was his pleasure. "Thank you for that. And you were in the right when you yelled at us. Now and on the phone. We came here on a whim for Beth, and I've not had any luck getting things squared away for us to live here with her."

"What sort of issues are you having? I'm assuming it's housing." She told him that was it. "Buying or renting? The reason I ask is, my family has both sitting empty right now."

"Buying. But you don't have to go to any trouble for us. We'll get it settled up." Joanie told her to shut up and let him help. He noticed they were doing the same thing he'd been doing, speaking and using sign language so that Beth could be a part of everything. "All right. We'll take your help. But you don't have to go out of your way and make your family—"

This time it was Beth that put her hand over her sister's mouth. She told him she'd take all the help he wanted to give them. She wasn't as stubborn or as stupid as her sisters.

Quincey laughed and called his brother Gunner. He knew he had several properties around town and could help these women out. Putting the phone on speaker when he asked his brother if it was all right, he explained who he was with as well as what they needed. He signed the conversation to Beth.

~*~

"I don't understand. What do you mean, he thinks one of us is his mate? I'm not going to settle down with someone that has to love me. No way." Grace looked at Beth as they spoke. "You have to have that wrong. He never said a word about it."

"Perhaps because you were so caustic to him the entire time he was trying to have lunch with me. You do understand that I'm an adult the same as you and Joanie are, don't you? I mean, I voted in the last election. I get to make my own money. All kinds of stuff." She told her sister to be nice. "No, I won't be nice to you. He was the perfect gentleman, despite the fact that I knocked him to the ground when he saved me from following that man into traffic. I hope he's not either of your mate. I'm positive he can do so much better than you guys."

After her sister left her, she stared at the work she'd been doing when the call had come in. Not that she didn't know each and every line she'd drawn. Standing up, she stood over the drawing without seeing it anymore. All she could think about was how rude and bitchy she'd been to Quincey. Both her and Joanie had been. Making a decision, she grabbed her keys and told Joanie where she was going. Joanie asked if she could go as well. All three of them ended up going to find Doctor Bishop.

The houses along his street were houses she'd always had an attraction for. The last two houses she'd drawn had been the same sort of antebellum homes. As soon as his driveway came up, the house sitting far back from the road, she knew this man was a smart businessman. The house, along with the garden out front and the grounds, was well maintained.

Getting out of the car, she was shocked to her core when a large white tiger came running at them from the side of the house. The larger than life cat stopped not a foot from where she was standing. She looked up at the house when a woman in a white apron asked if she wanted the doctor.

"No. Not unless he tries to eat me. I'm assuming this is Quincey Bishop?" The woman laughed and made her way toward them. "I came to talk to him about my behavior earlier today. Is he going to hurt me?"

"I'd say not. But he is Doc. He wants me to tell you that you and your sisters are welcome to go inside the house, but he has to go to the barn to change into clothing. He'll be naked should he shift right now." The cat snarled at the woman, who told him to behave himself. "I just baked up some zucchini bread if you'd like some. The garden out back is just plum full of the little suckers."

When the woman turned, heading back to the house, Joanie and Beth joined her. When Grace started to move to join them, the cat blocked her path. After he blocked her twice more, she stood where she was.

"I'm assuming you want me to stay here. I can do that. So long as you understand, I'm not going to let you hurt me. Or my sisters." She thought of what Beth said to her about being mates. "Am I your mate? I don't even know if you can understand me or not."

Her cell phone ringing nearly gave her a heart attack. Grace wasn't sure, but she thought Quincey was laughing at her. Answering the call from Joanie, she was laughing hard enough that it took her two tries to tell her why she'd call at this time.

"He said for you to put out your hand so he can nip it. Beth said it wasn't at all painful, but he can talk to you after he tastes your blood. I'd do it, Grace. What harm could it do for you to be able to speak to a tiger when you need one?"

She didn't ask her how she thought she'd

need him but put out her hand. The lick across her entire palm made her realize he was hiding a lot of teeth from her. When he nipped gently on her hand, she wasn't hurt at all. Pulling her hand back, noticing that it was still trembling a good deal, she asked him if it had worked.

It did. And yes, Grace, you're my mate. She nodded and looked away. *I won't hurt you or your family. Not ever. I'll protect them with my life, as I will you.*

"I'm not asking for you to do that, Quincey. I'm a little overwhelmed right now." He told her he was sorry for adding to her stress. "I came here to tell you how sorry I was for snapping at you so much. I'd like to tell you I was having an off day, but I'm snappish to everyone lately. I hate my job. I hate my life, and I just want to crawl into a cave and never come out. Nothing seems to be going right."

Is there anything I can do to help you? Shaking her head, she looked at him. *I'll do whatever you need me to do, Grace. Just tell me what has you overwhelmed. I want to know. No, that's not nearly enough. I need to know.*

"I draw houses. Pretty pictures of them so people can hang them in their homes and be so proud of it. However, no one wants to see their house the way it really looks. They want me to make it look like something they'll never be able to achieve. Not without a great deal of money and about five hundred years." Quincey asked her if someone was disappointed in what she did for them. "Yes. They're suing me for drawing a house that looks just like the one they sent me pictures of. No big trees out front, like they thought I'd just know they wanted there. The broken-down fence wasn't fixed, and lord have mercy, I should have read their mind and just assumed they'd want the yellow shutters to be black and the house to be white, not pink. I kid you not, Quincey. It's the ugliest pink you've ever seen. But they're suing me for the house they had in their heads and not what they have."

I can help you with that. I have a great many contacts to look into it for you. Or I could hire you a good attorney if you don't already have one. She told him he was too nice. *Thank you.*

She laughed when he didn't tell her she was as well. She knew she'd not been. But when she pointed it out to him, he stood up. Thinking he was going to attack her or something now that he was growling low in his throat, she bumped her head when he told her to get down behind her car.

The car came out of nowhere and slid to a stop not a foot from her own car. Gravel sprayed everywhere and hit her against the back of her legs. Quincey didn't move from his position, but two men came out of the house then and leaned against the posts. She didn't have any idea who they might be, but she thought they were much too relaxed compared to Quincey's fur standing on edge and his stiff stance.

"You need something?" The men came down the stairs from the porch and made their way to the new arrival, sauntering in a slow walk. "I asked you something, Mr. Jacobson. You'll live longer if you answer me and put that gun away."

"He said it was suicide. That brother of yours, he told the police he'd seen my son jump into the front of that moving truck on purpose. He needs to take that back. Right now." The sharp noise of a gun going off had her crying out, but she didn't move when Quincey told her she was all right. "Where is he? Where's Doc Bishop? I know he lives around here."

"You need to calm down and put that rifle away before you get hurt." Mr. Jacobson pointed out that he was the one holding the rifle. "You are at that, but that tiger right there is going to kill you if you don't calm down and put the rifle into your car. We'll talk to you then, but not with you waving that thing around like you've no idea who or what you're going to kill with it."

Someone else pulled into the drive, and she was afraid it was reinforcements for Mr. Jacobson. A woman and a man got out of the car and walked toward the elderly man. The woman was dressed in business attire, the man in a suit. The other two men nodded at them when they were next to her car.

"It's William, isn't it?" The man said he was, then told the woman talking that his son didn't commit suicide. "But he did. You know me, William. You know what I can do. I helped you a couple of weeks ago to find the paperwork your wife put up. I showed you what I can do, didn't I?"

"You speak to the dead." Grace could hear the grief in the other man's voice. "You got him there with you, Sasha? My son, he with you right now?"

"He is, and he wants to speak to you. Are you ready to see him? He's not able to glamour himself because of him only being dead for a few hours. Are you ready for what he looks like?" He said he wasn't, but he would like to see him. "All right."

"Oh, Billy. Oh my, Billy. What did they do to you?" Standing up, she stared at the man. It hurt her heart to see him like this. William went to his knees and asked over and over who had killed him. "You're all I have in the world, son. Did they take you from me?"

"No, Dad. No one took me from you. I did kill myself."

The sobbing was painful to hear. Before she could think what a dangerous thing she was doing, she made her way to the grieving man and took the gun from him. Then she held him to her breast as he cried for his loss.

"You're going to hear a lot of things about me, Dad, and most of them are going to be true. The woman I was seeing, however, is going to tell you the child she is carrying is mine. It's not. However, if you could see your way to do it, I'd very much like it if you could find someone to care for him. Otherwise, she'll sell him to someone, and you'll never see him."

"I'll raise him myself, Billy." Billy told his dad he didn't want that. He knew his dad had failing health. "You left me, son. I don't care what others are going to say. You left me here all alone."

"Dad, I was dying anyway. You knew that. The doctor I saw this morning, not Doc Bishop, but the guy I've been seeing said my cancer had advanced, and I didn't have but a few weeks to live. I couldn't let you do that, go through that again like you did with Mom." He said he would have. "I know you would have. I know that, Dad. But I didn't want you to have to. So I ended it."

William sobbed, his body becoming weaker with each passing moment. When Billy said he had to go, it was all Grace could do not to demand that he stay. When he was gone, she held onto William tightly, knowing some of his grief like her own.

"Grace?" She looked up at the man who'd been on the porch. "I'm Wesley, one of Quincey's brothers. This is Gunner, and Chandler is standing over with his wife, Sasha. Quincey asked us to take you inside, and one of us will drive Mr. Jacobson home. All right?"

"Will he be all right?" Wesley said his dad was going to stay with him tonight and help him with arrangements in the morning. "He's hurting very badly. I hurt for him."

"We all do. Come on now, honey. Let's get you into the house, and Quincey said he'd join you in a few minutes." Being led into the house, she stumbled a couple of times on the way up the stairs. "Steady there. You get hurt, and he's going to have my head. I'll get you settled and call your sisters for you."

As soon as she was seated, both her sisters came to sit with her. Grace was numb. She didn't know what had happened with the man and his son, but she did hurt for them both. Not that she'd not thought the same thing over the years. Her mother had been arrested and put away. Everyone looked at the three of them like they might go off the handle, too, killing any and everyone that got into their way.

When Quincey joined them in the living room, he sat across from them. She thought she could really love a man like him.

Chapter 8

Jamie watched his parents. He'd not thought of Dwayne as anything else but his father for the last few days. Today they were in the courtroom for them to get married. Now it was his turn to be adopted by the best dad he'd ever met. While nervous, he only had to look around to know he wasn't just getting a dad, but an entire family that loved him too. The judge said he had a few questions to ask him.

"Your Honor, I know you have a certain way you like to do things, but I want you to know that whatever you're planning to ask me, I've thought of it too. Am I sure? Yes. With all my heart, I'm sure I want to be a Bishop and son to Dad here. Do I think they'll care for me? You've no idea how many rules they've laid down that

I'm going to have to follow, and you know what? I love them and the rules. It means they care." The judge told him he thought he was getting into the best family. "I know that. Grandpa Saul is going to take me fishing next summer. Grandma Sippy is showing me how to cook. She said all men should know how to do that. I have uncles that are wonderful to me. They have all taken me into their family with open arms. I have a lot of cousins and aunts too. I'm about the luckiest kid in the world."

"You have thought about this a great deal, then." Jamie told the judge that being adopted had been in his mind since Dad had brought it up to him. "And what are you going to do with this newfound love, young man? I expect to never see you in my courtroom unless it's a good thing. Like you're an attorney, or you're getting married."

"I won't promise you I won't be here, but I can tell you that if I need to be standing in front of you as a judge, any one of my aunts will make whatever my sentence is seem minor. They're very strict on following the rules." The judge laughed. Everyone else did too. "My mom and I have just had each other for a long time, sir. Just waiting on Dad to come along and fall in love with us. I'm glad he didn't wait too long and find us when I was too old to appreciate having a good family."

"You see that you cherish these moments you've been given for the rest of your life, Jamie." He promised him he would. "Good. I see no reason to hold you all up any longer. Jamison Bishop, let me be the first to welcome you to your new family."

They were headed back to their house when it hit him that he was a Bishop. He had a family. His mom was happy and in love. While he wasn't sure why anyone would love a girl, he was all right with Dwayne loving his mother. He'd never seen her so happy.

Going up to his room to change, he looked around his room. It was perfect. Not only did he have a computer that he was using for homework and stuff, but he had a fish and several plants in his room. Pulling off his suit, he was hanging it back up when Molly knocked on his open door. She asked him how it felt to be a Bishop.

"Amazing. Just like you said it would be. Dad and Mom are married too." He sat down at his desk and she on his bed. "We're cousins now, I guess. Did you know that your GGMa invited me to go on a cruise with you and her?"

"You're stalling. Did you tell them?" He shook his head. "Why not, Jamie? You're going to have to tell them sooner rather than later. You've been practicing with your magic, haven't you?"

"Yes. I'm getting a lot better about it too. Also, I discovered something by accident." He got up and handed her an unopened bottle of water. "Go ahead, drink out of it. I made it just for you."

She unscrewed the lid, taking what he thought was too long to do it, and then took a small sip. Encouraging her to drink a big drink, she did after rolling her eyes at him. They both watched as the bottle not only refilled but also had a brand new lid on it.

"Jamie? Did you drink out of this to trick me?" He told her no, shocked that she'd even think such a thing about him. "How did you make this work? I'm sure it's different than just simply drawing it on your skin."

"I used a magic marker to draw it. Last night I was working on a project for class, and I got really thirsty. I only had a pencil and a magic marker on the desk, so I drew a bottle of water on my arm with the marker. The bottle came off my arm, and I set it there on my desk so I could finish one thing before I drank it. As soon as I finished off about half the bottle, it filled up again. Not only that, but it's freezing cold all the time." She drank more of her water after removing the lid. "Put the lid in the trash can. There is something else I need to show you."

As soon as she tossed the lid into the can by his desk, he showed her the can. The lid was gone. She even moved the other scraps of paper around to look for it. When she put it back, setting the bottle on the desk, they both watched it as it filled to the top and a new lid popped onto it.

"That is way cool. I did wonder about all the extra lids when you took one off, and it reappeared like on the bottle. But this is better than the cookies you made the other day when I was here." He said he was nervous. "Why? They knew you'd get some sort of magic from them helping you. You have this amazing ability that will keep you hydrated, and the earth clean too. Also, if you're ever someplace without food and water, you won't die from starvation."

"Are you always this cheery?" She laughed when he did. Jamie really was nervous. "Will you go with me to tell them? I'd feel a lot better if you were there. That way, when they call me a freak, I can go home with you. Aunt Raven will raise me, won't she?"

"I think she loves you more than me. But that won't happen. You're going to be just fine and dandy, as Grandpa Saul says all the time." Deciding that now was as good a time as any, they both headed down the stairs to the dining room where his mom was working on her computer. She claimed that the light was better in there. Jamie thought it was because she was in the center of the house and could see everything.

"Aunt Brit, Jamie has something to tell you and Uncle Dwayne. I have to go. See you later, Jamie."

He was going to murder her. It took him a second to realize his mom was talking to him. Turning to her, she smiled, and he thought that after killing his cousin, he was going to hug his mom before he would gladly go off to prison.

Dad joined them a few minutes after that and brought with him some summer sausage, cheese, and crackers. After nibbling on a cracker, he decided the best way to do this was to just show them. Picking up his mom's pen, he explained as he drew cookies on his arm.

"I, quite by accident, discovered something a few days ago." Mom told him not to write on his skin and offered him a sheet of paper. "No, this is important. Besides, it'll be gone in a few minutes. Anyway, I was making notes the other day on a test that was coming up. And before you ask, no, I wasn't making a cheat note for myself. I wrote this so that I'd have a hint on where to start on the—not that it matters. But I realized I could do this."

Touching the cookies on a plate he'd drawn, he peeled the drawing off and put it on the table. It changed from a drawing to a plate of cookies instantly. Also, even as small as he drew it, the plate and the cookies were about the same size as the ones he got from the kitchen when he wanted a snack.

They were only staring at the plate. Picking up one of the treats, he bit down on it, crumbs going everywhere. When Dad asked him how it tasted, Jamie laughed, then handed him the other half of his cookie.

"You didn't ask me how I'd done that but only asked me how it tasted. I thought for sure that one or both of you would have freaked out." They both looked at his mom. "Mom? Are you all right? I didn't know how else to tell you other than to just show you."

"I was just thinking of all the ways this would help you. I mean, we have a lot of money.

Someone could kidnap you, and I'd not have to worry about you being starved. Can you only make cookies?" He drew a sandwich. When he picked up her magic marker that she forever had, she put her fingers over his hand just as he was getting ready to draw. "If you draw a gun on your arm to use or a knife, I will beat you. I know I've threatened you many times before with that and never followed through, but I will if you ever draw a weapon."

"I might need to save you." She stared at him for several seconds, then nodded. "This one is a little hard to digest. I used my lazy brain to discover this."

"Lazy brain?" Jamie told Dad what a lazy brain was. He laughed. "All right. I guess that makes sense. You think of ways of getting something done with less work or energy, and that is your lazy thought process. I think we all use that on occasion."

After doing the same thing he'd done for Molly, he watched them digest what he'd been able to do. Mom didn't touch either the cookies or the drink, but Dad was munching on a cookie as he examined the bottle. Finally, after he seemed satisfied with it, he opened it and drank down more than half of it. Laughing as it refilled and a lid was put on it, he showed him how the first lid disappeared so as not to litter.

"You should have known we'd not be upset with you about this." He nodded at his dad when he said that. Mom had gone to take a phone call about something she was working on. "You were, weren't you? Afraid that we'd kick you to the curb or something equally dumb. We love you, Jamie. Nothing you could do like this would ever make us upset. I am glad, however, that you were able to go to Molly with it. It's nice to have someone around your own age that you can have a secret with. I did with my brothers too."

"Molly said you'd think it was special. I wasn't so sure. Mom hates it when I write on my skin. She said it's an ugly thing to have to cover up if you can't wash it off in the tub. Molly said the same thing Mom did, but she was more violent about it. She's weird." Dad just laughed, but he had a look that reminded him of Grandpa Saul. "Did Mom tell you about the email she got from her dad? I thought he was dead. I think she did too."

"She did. He needs cash. Did she tell you what he needed it for?" Jamie said she'd not. "He's wanting to come and see her, but he's been unemployed for some time. According to him, he just wants to see her and you now that he knows about you. I'm supposing you've never met him."

"No. Mom's mom killed herself when she was a little girl. Did she tell you?" Dad started to nod, then answered him. "She hates it when people nod. I guess she told you that."

"Yes. Several times." Dad laughed. "I'm having someone look into his sudden appearance. I'm thinking he read something in the newspaper about her marrying me, and that's how he found out where we were living. I want you to be careful with this new ability of yours. While we're on the subject, have you tried to draw money?"

"No. Do you think it might be something that he makes me do if Mom doesn't give him any money?" Dwayne said it was always smart to be ahead of someone that wanted money from you. "I guess you're right on that. I don't think she will give him any money. I don't think they were like you are with your parents."

"I don't think there are very many families like mine, do you?" Jamie said he was probably right. Then he picked up the pen again and drew what he hoped looked like paper money. "Just make it a one dollar bill for starters. We don't want to have to explain to anyone how come you're suddenly carrying around hundred dollar bills."

It worked. Not only did he have a dollar bill that he had made, but he was able to make coins too. Dad pointed out that if there was ever a payphone around, he'd have the money to make a call. Jamie had no idea what he was talking about but let it go. Something old people knew about, he supposed.

Feeling better after telling his parents, Jamie went to his room. He'd not been sleeping well. At first, it was nightmares about someone else being able to use his skin for things he didn't approve of. But after a quick test with Molly, they discovered not only did other people writing on him not work, but nothing anyone else wrote on him even showed up. He slept better that one night. Then the things he drew on his skin came to get him. Jamie hadn't ever thought of drawing tanks or even guys on his body until that night. Those things attacked him too. It got to the point he was afraid to close his eyes for fear of what would come after him.

Lying down on his bed, he closed his eyes. All was right with the world, he thought. He wasn't in trouble. His parents knew about the things he could do, and now he was safe. Jamie didn't even let the thought of his mom's dad interfere with his thoughts right now. Whoever it was and whatever he wanted, he was barking up the wrong tree with his family.

~*~

"What do you want, Dad? You've been out of my life for the last twenty years. Making it so that I had to grow up in the system, you never once came back to get me. Now all of a sudden, you not only want me to give you some money, but to welcome you back into my life?" George didn't get the opportunity to speak before she was on the warpath again. "I have a wonderful life in the event you were wondering. A son and a husband that I love dearly. Also, a family. A real one that supports one another."

"I'm a grandda again?" She said she was a mom, not that he was a grandda. "I don't think it works that way, honey. When you become a mom, that means I'm a grandda. But I'm getting off the subject. I don't need a lot of money, Brit. Just enough to make my way out to you. I just heard about Bree, and I wanted to go to her gravesite. To.... I missed so much. I've been pushing people away since your mom took her life."

"She was murdered, did you hear that? She and her two children and Howard." He said he'd read about it in the newspaper. "His father murdered them all because he could, Dad. Just put them into a storage container and filled it with enough poison gas that it killed them all. How could anyone do that?"

"There are a lot of monsters in the world, Brit. A lot of them look like everyday people too. But they show you sometimes. They just snap, and there the monster is." He thought about his own wife then. Margaret had been the worst kind of monster. Thinking of his daughters had had him looking for them. It had broken him when he'd read that Bree had been killed. "If you could see your way to getting me out there, I promise I won't bother you one bit while I'm there. If that's what you want. As much as I'd like to see your son, I won't do that to either of you if you're set on it. Please? Brit, I have nothing left but my memories, and they're so old. Could you see your way to letting me see this one thing?"

She was quiet for a while. He thought he might be smarter to just hang up and hitchhike his way out to Ohio. It would be cold going, he supposed. Ohio was one of the states that had all the seasons. Being in New Mexico all this time, he'd forgotten all about seasons. When she asked him where he was staying, he told her he didn't have an address.

"Where are you living, Dad? Not on the streets, are you?" He said he'd been living that way for so long he didn't know if he could live with four walls anymore. "I'll get you a ticket and have it at the airport. Do you have identification to be able to prove who you are?"

"I'm short on funds, honey. I don't have a car either. Figured there was no point in keeping it up if I couldn't drive."

She asked him to hold on.

George had been so excited when she'd accepted the reverse charges from the phone call. Trying to call her for days now, he'd been relieved when the phone company had been able to give him her business number. George had expected her to be working, but the name of the company had thrown him a bit. Uncollectable Merchandise sounded like a trash company. But he wasn't going to complain. If she'd help him this one time, he'd be forever grateful to her. Even if she didn't want to see him or allow him to see his grandson.

"All right. There will be a private jet on the

runway at the airport. All you need to do is have someone take a picture of you and send it to me. Do you know anyone with a cell phone, Dad?" He said he did, and he'd do that. Then she gave him the phone number where to send it. "That's my personal cell number. When you arrive, I want you to call me and let me know that you've made it. I'll come there and pick you up."

"Will you be bringing your husband and son?" She told him she'd bring Jamie, but maybe not Dwayne. He was working. "Of course he is. I should have guessed that. I'll send it as soon as I get to see my buddy. He's got a nice phone that he uses. I'll do it here within an hour. I can't thank you enough for this, Brit. I've got a lot of explaining to do, and I hope you'll let me say it."

"We'll see, Dad. It's been a long time. And up until you called me the other day, I thought you'd died a long time ago. This is something we're going to have to take one day at a time. All right?" He didn't tell her that every day he'd thought he would die—he'd keep that part to himself. "I'll see you when you get here."

It was more than he could have hoped for. He was going to get to see his daughter after all this time. And he had himself another grandson. The other two, like Brit's, he'd not known about.

George had been keeping himself a low profile for a very long time. It was only a month ago when he was told he'd be able to go back home. That it was finally over about his wife and her drama.

George hadn't always wanted to find his children. Just being able to be away from their mother had been more than enough for him. Millicent had been a horror. And a whore. But it was her drinking and drugs that had been such a surprise to him.

Then one night, the two of them had had the fight of all fights. Never had he ever hit her, but she'd beaten him with anything she could put her hands on. Not that he was a pussy or anything like that. George had been a large man back then and a fighter too. He'd been so afraid to even hug her too tightly for fear of hurting her. So he'd allowed her to take her frustrations and anger out on him. George had never wanted her to hurt the girls.

Then one night, she had. His taking Brit to the hospital had pissed her off. But she'd hurt her so badly, and her only being a little thing, that she'd ended up spending four days and nights there. George had never left her side, Bree lying right in the bed next to her sister so he could keep an eye on them both. That had been the end of him covering for her.

Taking the girls to fights with him had been all right at first. He had a good manager that kept an eye on them while he was in the ring. After the fights, he'd take them back to his hotel room, giving them whatever they wanted for being such good girls. But then Millicent accused him of abusing them, sexually as well as physically. Before he could get arrested, if that had been the plan, Millicent had hung herself.

George found his buddy Cutter and asked him to send a picture of himself to his little girl. That made the older man laugh, thinking, he was sure, that George was lying. But he snapped his picture, then sent it on to the phone number Brit had given him. The ball, as they said, was in her court now.

Going back to his cubby hole, he looked around at the things he'd collected over the years to see what he was going to need to take with him. He'd kept very little from his time with his family, just a single picture of the girls when they'd been four and three. Kissing their little faces as he did every night, George thought about his fleeing New York as he made his way to the airport to be picked up.

The police had contacted him at the hotel to tell him that Millicent had killed herself. He'd been shocked by the news. George's first thought was that Chappy, his manager, had killed her when he heard she'd tried to kill Brit. But they'd told him she hung herself. Another thing that didn't ring true with his wife. Not only was she vain, but she wasn't one to do anything that required her to work very much. Hanging herself seemed like a great deal of work to him. But like other things he'd found out about his wife, he kept them to himself.

Then they'd taken his daughters from him. It wasn't much longer before they told him that he was a suspect in Millicent's murder. Unable to find his children, not sure what their thinking was, he'd left the state and traveled as far as the money he'd had on him would take him. He'd been living off the grid since then.

While waiting on someone to come around and pick him up, George found a nice secluded place to take himself a nap. There had been a nice-sized piece of cardboard there, too, so he curled up in it and closed his eyes.

Waking up with the bright sun blinding him for several seconds, he was startled when someone called his name. He wasn't sure who it was, so he said nothing as the man's voice got closer and closer to where he was. Suddenly the piece of cardboard he'd found at the airport was knocked upon, and he laid as still as he could until the man spoke again.

"My name is Dwayne Bishop. My wife, your daughter, sent me here to find you. While you are difficult to find, I'm assuming on purpose, Mr. Handle, I want you to know I'm not human, and I found you by your scent. I'm glad you waited here at the airport, or I might well have had some trouble finding out where you were before here." George came out of his newest home and stood up. "Hello there, Mr. Handle. As I said, my name is Dwayne. I'm here to take you to my home."

Not sure the man would understand how much his words meant to him, George hugged the man tightly. Just as he realized how stupid he was being, the man hugged him back, as tightly as he needed, too. Stepping back, he told him he was sorry.

"No need to be sorry. You're grateful that someone came for you, and I understand that. Do you have anything in there that you'd like to take back with you? I have some luggage for you if you have a lot." George told him all he had was a picture. "If you'd like to get it, you and I will have some breakfast and talk. Nothing bad, I assure you. But since we're related by way of Brit, I'd like to get to know you. Oh, I brought someone for you to meet. Jamie, this is your Grandda George. George, this is our son, Jamison Bishop."

For as much as he wanted to hug the young man, he didn't want to frighten him. "My middle name is Jamison. George Jamison Handle. I'm so very glad to meet you, Jamie. You look a great deal like your mother, I'm betting."

"Mom told me I look like you. She has a few pictures of you when you were a child. I didn't know about you. I'm sorry about that." George told him what Dwayne had told him, not to be sorry about meeting a stranger. "I'm starving. I bet you are too."

George was put into a large black limo. There were things in it for him to snack on, but he was just too nervous to partake of anything. He wasn't going to be sick in the beautiful car. Jamie and Dwayne told him what they were going to do while here. George asked about Brit.

"She got in a huge shipment just before we were scheduled to leave, or she would have come with us. Brit rents furniture and things like that to movie sets. Just recently, she purchased a lot of old cars that we're having sent to a place where she is storing things." George was impressed and told them that. "You should see her inventory. It's all organized by decade. She has an impressive inventory."

"You love her." When the younger man's face lit up, he could see that he did indeed love Brit. "How long have you been married? A while, I'm guessing."

"A few days, actually." He looked at Jamie, then back at him. "Jamie is my adopted son. I couldn't love him anymore if he was of my blood. But he and Brit came as a package deal, and I'm as happy as I've ever been. And so much in love that I can't believe I've been so lucky to have found her and Jamie."

After breakfast, they headed to the store. He wasn't one to steal things. He didn't need all that much. But having underwear as well as shoes and socks made him crave a nice hot shower too. As soon as he was about to ask for one, he was in a hotel room with Jamie. Dwayne had some business to attend to.

"He works for GGMa Holly as her secondhand man. Dad is here to look at a failing business that needs to borrow some money to expand. I'm not sure how it all works, but they help when they can, and Dad has no problem telling them that it won't work and walking away. GGMa Holly said that's what makes him a good business partner." He said he didn't understand it either. "Dad will come by to pick us up when he's finished. If he runs through lunch, he said you and I could go to the hotel restaurant and charge our meal to the bill. I'd count on that if I were you. These things always take forever."

"You don't like that?" Jamie told him he loved going with his dad, as he got to hang out around a pool and have strange food. "I guess there is that. I'm going to take a shower. You need anything. Just pound on the door."

As soon as he was under the hot spray, George let the tears flow. It was working out much better than he'd thought it would. He had a good son-in-law, a grandson, and he was going to see his daughter soon. His heart was so full that it ran right out of his eyes in the form of the happiest tears he'd ever shed.

Before You Go...

HELP AN AUTHOR

write a review

THANK YOU!

Share your voice and help guide other readers to these wonderful books. Even if it's only a line or two, your reviews help readers discover the author's books so they can continue creating stories that you'll love. Log in to your favorite retailer and leave a review. Thank you.

Kathi Barton, a winner of the Pinnacle Book Achievement award as well as a best-selling author on Amazon and All Romance books, lives in Nashport, Ohio, with her husband, Paul. When not creating new worlds and romance, Kathi and her husband enjoy camping and going to auctions. She can also be seen at county fairs with her husband, who is an artist and potter.

Her muse, a cross between Jimmy Stewart and Hugh Jackman, brings her stories to life for her readers in a way that has them coming back time and again for more. Her favorite genre is paranormal romance, with a great deal of spice. You can visit Kathi on line and drop her an email if you'd like. She loves hearing from her fans. aaronskiss@gmail.com.

Follow Kathi on her blog: http://kathisbartonauthor.blogspot.com/

www.ingramcontent.com/pod-product-compliance
Lightning Source LLC
LaVergne TN
LVHW091144080826
845145LV00008B/2253

* 9 7 8 1 9 5 5 0 8 6 6 9 1 *